Before she could reply, Brooke held up the stuffed animal. "Give Bunny a kiss goodbye, Daddy."

Jake's mouth dropped open an inch. "How about a high five?"

Her mouth set in a stubborn way that made Millie think of Jake. Already like father, like daughter. "A kiss."

He bent forward and touched his lips to the animal's grungy fur.

"Me, too," Brooke said, angling her cheek toward him.

He glanced up at Millie, emotion clouding his eyes. She nodded, the tingling in her body rapidly progressing to a full-on tremble.

Jake kissed his daughter's cheek then the top of her head. Millie wasn't sure if the sigh she heard came from her or the therapist waiting for him. Jake straightened and she noticed a faint color across his cheeks. The doctor was actually blushing. Why was vulnerability so darned appealing when it came wrapped up in an alpha male package?

Finding

SUDDENLY A FATHER

BY

MICHELLE MAJOR

Published in Great Britain 2015
by Mills & Boon, an imprint of Harlequin (UK) Limited,
Eton House, 18-24 Paradise Road, Richmond, Surrey, TW9 1SR

ISBN: 978-0-263-25144-9

23-0615

Harlequin (UK) Limited's policy is to use papers that are natural, renewable and recyclable products and made from wood grown in sustainable forests. The logging and manufacturing processes conform to the legal environmental regulations of the country of origin.

Printed and bound in Spain
by CPI, Barcelona

Michelle Major grew up in Ohio but dreamed of living in the mountains. Soon after graduating with a degree in journalism, she pointed her car west and settled in Colorado. Her life and house are filled with one great husband, two beautiful kids, a few furry pets and several well-behaved reptiles. She's grateful to have found her passion writing stories with happy endings. Michelle loves to hear from her readers at michellemajor.com.

For Lauren. You are amazing in so many ways—
mother, teacher and friend.
I'm lucky and grateful to have you as my sister.

Chapter One

Millie Spencer took a deep breath, wiped a few stray potato chip crumbs from her sundress and knocked on the door a second time.

As she waited, her eyes scanned the front porch of the large shake-shingle house, empty save for an intricate spiderweb inhabiting one corner. The wraparound porch practically begged for a wooden swing, where a person could sit on a late-summer afternoon sipping a glass of lemonade and watching the world go by. As a girl, Millie had longed for a place like that, but in the tiny condo she'd shared with her mother there'd been no room for any space of her own.

Still no one answered, so she rapped her knuckles against the door once more. This house sat at the edge of town in Crimson, Colorado, but only a few minutes from her sister's renovated Victorian near Crimson's center.

She was here as a favor to her sister—half sister—Olivia. Or was Olivia doing the favor for Millie? Millie'd shown up on Olivia's doorstop a few days ago, beaten down both emotionally and financially. To her relief, Olivia and her husband, Logan Travers, hadn't asked many questions, just welcomed Millie into their home. Up until today, Millie had spent most of her time curled on the couch watching bad reality TV and overdosing on junk food.

Now she was here, sent to help Logan's recently injured brother and his daughter. Except it appeared they weren't home. Which was weird, since Logan had said his brother, Jake, couldn't drive yet. It was a beautiful late-August day, so maybe the two had walked to the park Millie'd seen a few blocks over.

She was ready to leave when the door opened a crack. She could see a sliver of a man's face through the opening. "We don't want any," he said, peering down at her.

"Any what?" She leaned forward, trying to get a glimpse beyond him into the house. Curiosity almost always got the best of her.

"Cookies or popcorn or whatever you're selling," he answered quickly, glancing behind him before the eye she could see, a startlingly blue eye, tracked back to her again. It was the same blue as Logan's, so this must be the brother. "Do you have a parent with you?"

Her mouth dropped open and she pulled herself up to her full height, all five foot two. And a half. When she wore heels. "I'm not..." she began, but the man muttered a curse and disappeared into the house.

He hadn't shut the door when he'd turned away. She could still only see through the couple-inch slat, and without a second thought, she extended her foot and nudged the door open wider. She stretched forward but didn't step into the house. "Hello?" she called and her voice echoed.

The entry was devoid of furniture. Olivia had told

her Logan's brother had recently returned to Crimson, so maybe he had furnishings for his home on order. She hoped his purchases included a porch swing.

A sound reached her from the back of the house. Another curse and a child crying. She bit down on her lip and grabbed her cell phone from her purse, intending to call Olivia and Logan for backup. But the crying got louder, followed by a strangled shout of "no," and Millie charged forward, unable to stop herself.

She came up short as she entered the back half of the house. Rays of sunshine streamed through the windows, lighting the open family room as well as the kitchen beyond. Her gaze caught on the family room. Unlike the front of the house, the room looked furnished, although it was hard to tell because dolls, stuffed animals and an excess of pink plastic covered every square inch. It looked as if a toy store had thrown up all over the place. Did Jake Travers really have only one child? There was enough stuff here to keep a whole army of kids busy. She forced her eyes away from the girlie mess to the kitchen.

Two tall bar stools were tucked under the island, which was littered with cereal boxes and various milk and juice cartons. A mix of what looked like chocolate milk and grape juice spilled over the counter onto one of the stools and the tile floor, soaking a pile of soggy Cheerios from an overturned bowl.

Jake stood in the middle of the kitchen with his back to her. She noticed immediately that he was tall and broad, wearing a gray athletic T-shirt, basketball shorts that came almost to his knees and an orthopedic boot on his right leg that covered him from midcalf to foot.

He also sported a purple tutu around his waist. Despite the chaos of the situation, she almost smiled at that. No wonder he hadn't wanted to open the door for her.

In front of him, a little girl was crying and jumping up, grasping for a stuffed animal he held out to the side. It might have been a rabbit and was dripping more juice on the floor. The child had no hope of reaching it. Millie guessed he was well over six foot. When Olivia had sent her here to help Logan's poor, injured brother, Millie had pictured a debilitated invalid, not the hulking man before her.

She almost backed out of the room and fled, but at that moment the young girl's eyes met hers. They were the same shade of blue as her father's, so big they almost looked out of place on her heart-shaped face. Her hair was several shades darker than her father's, hung past her shoulders, and although she had the enviable natural highlights that children got, it looked as if it could benefit from a good brushing. She wore a pale pink leotard and matching tutu, the very essence of a tiny ballerina. Other than the juice stains down the front of it. Millie felt an immediate connection to her.

The child fell silent except for a tiny hiccup. Her eyes widened as she pointed at Millie. "It's a real life fairy."

Jake Travers breathed a sigh of relief before turning to see what his daughter, Brooke, was pointing at. He hardly cared if a real life fairy was standing in his house. It had stopped Brooke's crying and already the pounding in his head was starting to subside.

But it wasn't a fairy staring at him from the far side of the family room. The girl he'd tried to chase away minutes earlier held up a tentative hand and waved at him. Not a girl, he realized now. She was a woman, a tiny sprite of a woman, but the morning light silhouetting her body revealed the soft curves underneath her flowery flowing dress.

"I'm Millie," she said, nodding, as if willing him to understand her. "Millie Spencer. Olivia's sister? She and Logan sent me over." She tucked a strand of chin-length, caramel-colored hair behind one ear, the bracelets at her wrist tinkling as she moved.

Brooke let out an enraptured gasp. "Look, Daddy, she sparkles."

He narrowed his eyes as he set the dripping stuffed bunny onto the counter. Millie Spencer indeed appeared to be shimmering in the light.

She looked down at her bare arms and laughed, a sound just as bubbly and bright as the noise from her bracelets. "It's my lotion, sweetie," she said, taking a step forward. "I must have grabbed the one that glitters."

He watched his daughter's face light up. "I want glitters," she answered, her tone dreamy.

"You said Logan sent you?" Jake crossed his arms over his chest, careful of the splint that cradled his right hand. Glitter was the last thing he needed in this already chaotic house.

Millie scrunched up her pert nose. "I was under the impression Logan talked to you about me. That you need help because of..." She waved her hand up and down in front of him. More tinkling from the bracelets.

His back stiffened. Jake hated his injuries, how they'd changed his life and how out of control he felt these days. He vaguely remembered Logan calling last night to suggest babysitting help for Brooke and someone who could drive Jake to his physical-therapy and doctors' appointments. But Jake had been in the middle of burning a frozen pizza and had only half listened to his brother's well-meaning offer.

Jake didn't need help. At least he didn't *want* to need

help. Especially not from someone who looked as if her best friend was Tinker Bell.

"We're all good here."

She glanced around the room before her gaze zeroed in on his waist. "Are you sure about that?"

"We were having dance lessons," he mumbled as he pulled the crinkly tutu Brooke had insisted he wear down off his hips. He flicked it to the side and gave Millie a curt nod. He could handle this on his own. That was how he'd gotten by most of his life. He wasn't about to change now.

"I want glitters." Brooke tugged at the hem of his T-shirt.

He placed his uninjured hand on his daughter's head, smoothing back her long hair. His fingers caught on something that felt suspiciously like a wad of gum. Damn. He smiled and made his voice soft. "No glitter today, Brooke. Do you want to watch a show?"

Her mouth pinched into a stubborn line. "Glitters," she repeated then ducked away from his touch. "And Bunny." She grabbed the stuffed animal off the counter before he could stop her.

She squeezed the bunny to her chest. Jake couldn't stifle his groan as a trickle of purple liquid soaked her pink blouse. The last bit of command he had over his life seemed to seep away at the same time.

He turned back to Millie, but she'd disappeared.

Oh, no, he thought to himself. Not now when he was willing to admit defeat.

Lifting Brooke and Bunny against his chest with his good arm, he tried to ignore that his shirt was already soaking through. "Let's go find our fairy," he told his daughter and was rewarded with a wide grin.

Millie didn't stop when Jake Travers called her name. She concentrated on the warm sun and cool mountain breeze instead of her tumbling emotions. Even as a favor to Olivia, Millie had no intention of sticking around where she wasn't wanted. She made the mistake of turning around halfway through the yard when the little girl cried out.

Jake was struggling down the porch steps, his daughter clutched to his side as he balanced most of his weight on the nonbooted foot. "Are you really going to make me chase after you like this?" he asked as she met his gaze.

"I thought things were *all good*," she said as she retraced her steps toward the house.

He stood at the edge of the grass. "I'm used to taking care of myself. Needing help is a bit of a foreign concept."

"Everyone needs help from time to time."

He pursed his mouth into a thin line. "Not me."

Jake was clearly disconcerted by his current circumstances, and Millie felt a twinge of sympathy for him. She could spout platitudes about everyone needing help, but she'd been fending for herself long enough to understand his reluctance to rely on another person.

Before she could answer, Brooke squirmed in her father's arms and he reached out to steady her. Millie saw him wince as the girl's elbow jabbed into his splinted wrist. He lowered Brooke slowly to the ground and she clung to his leg. Millie noticed that liquid from the sopping wet stuffed animal had not only drenched his shirt, which now clung to a set of enviably hard abs, but a trail of wetness also leaked into the black orthopedic boot that covered his leg.

He didn't seem to notice, just stared at his daughter as if he wasn't sure how he'd ended up with a small child wrapped around him.

Millie cleared her throat and he looked up. "Sorry.

I haven't been a dad for very long. It's still sometimes amazing that she's really mine."

"How old are you, Brooke?" Millie asked, squatting down to the girl's level.

Brooke, suddenly shy, kept her gaze on her bunny but held up four fingers.

Millie glanced at Jake, her eyebrows raised.

"What did Logan and Olivia tell you about me?" he asked.

"Not much," she admitted. "That you're a surgeon who travels around the world. You were injured during an earthquake on an island near Haiti and need help with your daughter while you recover."

One side of his mouth curved. "That's an abbreviated version."

"So I gathered," Millie answered. She held out a hand to Brooke. "Sweetie, can I help you give Bunny a bath? She's dripping all over your daddy's leg."

"Bunny's a boy," Brooke and her father said at the same time.

Millie smiled. "He's not going to smell very good if that juice dries on him. How about we wash him off, then you can watch while he goes in the dryer?"

Brooke released the death hold she had on Jake's leg the tiniest bit. "He wants a bubble bath."

"Of course he does." Millie straightened and took a step forward, wiggling her fingers. "Can you show me the bathroom? We'll take good care of him."

With a tentative nod, Brooke took Millie's hand. This brought her only a few inches from Jake, who smelled like a strangely intriguing mix of grape juice and laundry detergent. "I'd like to understand the whole story," she said quietly.

He nodded, his deep blue eyes intent on hers. "I'll get

changed then explain it." He lowered his voice and added, "I'd rather not discuss the details in front of Brooke."

The little girl tugged her toward the house. "Bunny wants to smell good."

Millie started to follow but paused as Jake pressed his uninjured hand to her bare arm. She almost flinched but caught herself, focusing on the warmth of his fingers.

His hand lifted immediately. "I just wanted to say thank you."

"I haven't done anything yet."

He leaned in to whisper in her ear, "My daughter hasn't cried for the past fifteen minutes. You have no idea what an accomplishment that is."

Although she knew it meant nothing, Millie was surprised to feel a tiny kernel of happiness unfurl in her chest along with a shimmer of awareness for Jake Travers. Best to ignore the awareness and focus on the happiness. It had been so long since she'd accomplished anything of value in her life. She'd learned to appreciate even the smallest victory.

"It's going to be okay, Jake," she said, hoping beyond all reason that she could make it true for both of them.

Chapter Two

It took Jake longer than he wanted to get cleaned up, which was one more thing to add to his current list of frustrations. As a surgeon with Miles of Medicine, an international medical humanitarian organization, he was used to moving quickly. He'd made efficiency a priority in his life—in movement, time and, most important, relationships. He lived simply, able to pack up with an hour's notice based on where he was most needed.

The place he was most needed right now was in Brooke's life, but it galled him how inept and incapable he felt. He hadn't even bothered with a proper shower because the hassle of maneuvering himself in and out with his ankle and arm wasn't worth the trouble. Without the boot or splint, he couldn't put weight on his right leg or use his right arm. Instead he'd done his best to wash off the sticky juice residue in the master bath before dressing in his current uniform of a T-shirt and baggy shorts, the only clothes he could change into quickly despite his injuries.

The door to the guest bathroom was closed as he came down the hall. He was grateful his sister-in-law had found him a rental property with two bathrooms in the main part of the house so that Brooke could have her own space. He couldn't make out the words over the sound of running water but could hear her sweet voice rising and falling as she spoke to Millie Spencer.

Unwilling to deal with the reality of how much he needed help quite yet, he started the monumental task of cleaning the kitchen. He'd wiped down most of the counters and covered the floor with almost half a roll of paper towels before Millie followed Brooke into the room.

His daughter cradled Bunny in her arms in a fluffy towel. "Daddy, sniff." She held out the stuffed animal to him. "He smells so good."

He breathed deeply but all he got was a big whiff of wet fake fur. "That's nice," he told Brooke.

Millie grinned at him over Brooke's head. "Laundry room?"

"To your left just past the table."

She carried a small plastic stool in her hands. "Let's get Bunny dry, Brooke. You can watch him spin while your daddy and I talk."

To Jake's surprise, Brooke nodded. Since he'd brought his daughter to Crimson, the only time she would let him out of her sight was when she slept. Maybe Millie Spencer was some sort of kid whisperer. Jake sure as hell needed one.

"So you're Olivia's sister?" he asked as Millie walked back into the room a few minutes later.

When she nodded, he added, "You two don't look alike."

"She's actually my half sister. We have the same dad."

"Did you grow up together?"

Her shoulders stiffened even as she gave him a gentle smile. "I'm guessing we only have a few minutes before your daughter gets bored watching the dryer. Is this really how you want to use that time?" She crouched down and began cleaning the paper towels from the floor.

"You don't have to do that. It's my mess."

She didn't stop to look at him. "Tell me about you and Brooke."

When her chin-length hair fell into her face, she didn't bother to push it away. He wanted to reach out himself, to see if the caramel-colored strands were as soft as they looked. The skin on her arms looked just as smooth, although he noticed how toned they were as she wiped up the spill.

"I first learned that I had a daughter two months ago." He continued straightening the kitchen as her attention remained on the floor. Somehow the fact that both of them kept busy made it easier to tell the story. "Brooke's mother was a doctor I knew from my travels, another aid worker. We were only together a few times when our paths crossed in the field. Then Stacy disappeared." His fingers gripped the cup he'd just picked up so hard the plastic began to bend. He released his hold and loaded the cup into the dishwasher. "She found me where I was working near Haiti a couple of months ago to tell me I had a four-year-old daughter back in Atlanta who was asking about her father. Stacy wanted to give me a chance to be a part of Brooke's life."

"That must have been a real shock." Millie stood and threw the wad of paper towels into the garbage.

Jake thought about her observation as he watched her

wet a dish towel and begin wiping down the tile floor around the spill. "You *really* don't have to do that."

"It will be sticky otherwise," she answered. "Keep talking, Jake."

He hated this part of the story and the guilt and helplessness that went with it. Jake had spent most of his childhood feeling helpless to stop the damage his father caused in their family, and when he'd finally broken free, guilt over the siblings he'd left behind had become his replacement companion.

He'd never expected to return to Colorado, but it was the only real home he'd ever known. The fact that both of his brothers had settled in Crimson and seemed happy with their lives was part of why he'd brought Brooke to his hometown. For a few brief moments when he'd first arrived, he'd hoped this place would have some special effect on him. But he'd only felt overcome by memories and more trapped than when he'd been injured.

His family understood enough of what had happened that they didn't ask questions he couldn't answer. "I was shocked, to say the least. I'd never planned on having kids. My work is my life. Being a dad wasn't part of the master plan. But I didn't have time to think about what I wanted. Stacy and I argued and she left the hospital late at night. We'd been down there just a few days because of an earthquake and I'd been running on too much coffee and too little sleep. I didn't even get a chance to process what she'd told me, but I followed her to the hotel. Once we got inside, there was an aftershock almost as big as the original. The roof of the hotel caved in, and she was killed."

Millie straightened once more, shock evident on her face. "Brooke's mother died?"

He gave a curt nod. “She should have never come down there like that. Things were too unstable.”

“It was a big risk.”

He looked past her, his guilt weighing so heavily that he finally had to explain in detail how he’d destroyed so many lives. “Stacy had called and emailed me over the course of several months. I thought she wanted to get together again and was avoiding her. I left her no choice but to track me down. In the end, I couldn’t help her because I was pinned under the rubble of the building. I held her hand in those last moments, but that’s all.” He gingerly crossed his arms over his chest. “Her parents were taking care of Brooke, but Stacy made me promise to look after her. She left custody to me, a man who didn’t even know his own daughter.” He shook his head, still unable to believe the events that had brought him here. “I had surgery on my wrist and ankle and then went to find Brooke.”

“The grandparents were willing to let her go?”

“For now.” He clenched his uninjured fist. “Brooke didn’t hesitate, which was the craziest part. Stacy had talked about me, had told Brooke she was going to find her father. My picture was in a frame on Brooke’s nightstand. I walked into their house in Atlanta, and she reached for me as if I’d been her dad forever. Like she’d been waiting for me.”

“Kids can be pretty amazing,” Millie whispered.

“I don’t know the first thing about being a dad, but I owe it to that little girl and her mother to try. Stacy’s parents still want to raise Brooke. I’m not sure what’s going to happen—there’s some nerve damage to my hand and it’s questionable whether I’ll be able to go back to my old job.”

“But you won’t leave Brooke?”

He heard the unspoken accusation in her tone and almost welcomed it. Everyone he knew had been tiptoeing around his future since he'd come back to the States. "I want what's best for her. You saw me today. It's highly unlikely that I'm it."

"You're her father." Color flushed bright in Millie's cheeks. "You can't desert her now that she depends on you."

He shrugged. "I'm in way over my head here."

"I can help," she answered immediately.

Jake could feel that tension radiated through her, an edginess at odds with her pixie haircut, hippie-girl sundress and shimmering skin. "Why do you want to help?" he asked, taking a step toward her. "What's your story, Millie Spencer?"

A sliver of panic flashed in her eyes before she regulated her gaze. "I've worked at both elementary and preschools, but I'm between jobs. I'm almost finished with a degree in early childhood education and am taking a break from classes, which is why I came to visit Olivia. We didn't grow up together, so we're just getting to know each other. She invited me to Crimson while I have some free time. Getting to know someone and mooching off them for several months are two different things. I need a job while I'm here, and I'm great with kids."

"Do you have references?"

"Of course. Although I just saved the beloved Bunny and cleaned your kitchen floor. I'd say that's a pretty good reference for myself."

He held up his hands, his right arm difficult to hold out straight. "Like I said, being a dad is new to me. I want to make sure I do the right thing for Brooke."

She nodded, as if she approved of his answer. "I have

a list of references in my car. I'll get it before I leave. Is Brooke in preschool?"

He rubbed his hand across his face then pointed to a pile of papers stacked on a nearby desk. "Registration is on the to-do list. I can't believe how wiped out I am by the time she goes to bed."

"I can help," Millie repeated.

"I can't drive yet and have regular physical-therapy and doctor appointments."

"That's fine, too." Her posture relaxed. "Olivia offered me the apartment above her garage. She and Logan live pretty close, so I can be here whenever you need."

He shook his head. "There's a guest suite off the family room toward the back of the house. You can stay there."

Her eyes widened. "That's not…"

"Look at me." He shifted on his bad leg. "I can't drive. Hell, I can barely bend down to pick something off the floor. If anything happens to Brooke, I want to make sure you're close."

He didn't mention the blistering relief he already felt at not being solely in charge of keeping his daughter alive. Jake had managed through a lot of high-stakes situations, but nothing had scared him like the responsibility of fatherhood. He hadn't realized how much it weighed on him until the possibility of Millie presented itself.

She continued to frown.

"I'm harmless," he said, flashing his most convincing smile.

Millie's eyes rolled in response. "Hardly."

"I'm desperate," he said softly.

Her smile was gentle and genuine. "That I believe. Are you sure this is a good idea?"

"Nothing about my life is good at the moment but…"

His voice trailed off as Brooke walked back into the kitchen.

"The dryer dinged," she said, bouncing up and down on her toes. "Is Bunny ready?"

"Nothing?" Millie asked.

"One good thing," he amended. "She's the only bright spot I have. I'm going to make things right for her." He looked at his daughter. "What would you think about Millie becoming your nanny and helping with things around the house?"

"She's Mary Poppins," Brooke yelled happily. Her eyes widened as she turned to Millie. "Will you bring the glitters?"

"Of course." Millie smiled then glanced at Jake, her expression wry. "I'm not quite Mary Poppins, but we've got a deal."

"Are you kidding me?" Millie yelled as she burst through the back door of her sister's house thirty minutes later. "Next time you should mention that you're sending me into pure chaos before I get there."

Olivia Travers stood on the far side of the island in the oversize kitchen. She shrugged her shoulders and tried, but failed, to hide the small smile that curved the corner of her mouth. "Would you have gone if I'd explained the whole story to you?"

"Gone where?" the woman sitting on one of the bar stools asked.

Millie recognized Olivia's friend Natalie Holt from the last time she'd been in Crimson. A tiny pang of jealousy stabbed at her heart for the life Olivia had made in this quaint Colorado mountain town. Millie had never been great at cultivating friendships.

"To Jake's." Olivia drummed her nails in a nervous rhythm on the granite counter. "What happened?"

Natalie swiveled in her chair. "Yes, what happened? Jake was always my favorite of the Travers brothers. Tall, blond and wicked smart."

"Well, now he's tall, blond and a hot mess," Millie answered, omitting the part about how terrified he seemed of failing his daughter.

"Emphasis on *hot*, I imagine." Natalie nabbed a chocolate chip cookie from the plate on the counter. "Want one?" she asked Millie.

"Did Logan make them?" Millie asked, inching forward, temporarily distracted by her unwavering devotion to all things chocolate.

Olivia nodded and pushed the plate toward Millie. "I'm sorry, Mill. But he needs help. I knew you'd be able to get through to him. Logan and Josh are worried."

"Then why is he alone with his daughter?" Millie couldn't help the recrimination in her voice. "What kind of family leaves someone in his condition to fend for himself?"

"What condition?" Natalie made a face. "I didn't even know Jake was in town. Why am I always the last to know everything?"

"Sorry," Olivia answered. "Jake wanted some privacy until he got settled."

"Whatever." Natalie reached out to pat Millie's arm. "You're new around here, Millie, so let me explain how hard it is to stay mad at Saint Olivia. She's just too damn sweet."

"Tell me about it," Millie muttered, scooting forward to take a cookie. Logan was a phenomenal baker, even if she questioned his skills as a brother.

"Have a seat," Natalie said, patting the chair next to

her. "I don't have to pick up my son for another hour and I'm guessing whatever's happening with Jake is way more interesting than any bad reality TV that's on at the moment." She looked between Olivia and Millie. "Who wants to spill it? You know I'm not going to tell anyone."

Olivia sighed. "Jake was injured while on a medical mission near Haiti, an aftershock from a big earthquake. At the same time, he discovered he had a four-year-old daughter." Natalie's mouth dropped open, but Olivia continued, "The girl's mother died when a hotel roof collapsed but had granted him custody. So he's brought Brooke to Crimson while he recovers. She's adorable and totally dependent on him. He's working with an orthopedic surgeon he knows at the hospital between here and Aspen. It's a renowned sports medicine center and I guess he has some friends there. At this point, they're not sure if he has permanent nerve damage in his right hand or what exactly the injuries mean for his surgical career."

"I can't believe you didn't tell me any of that," Millie said.

"I thought it would be better if Jake explained the situation," Olivia said quietly. "And I wanted you to meet Brooke before you said no to working for him."

"Because I'm a sucker for kids." Millie broke the cookie in half and popped the whole thing in her mouth, chewing furiously. "I'm a total sucker."

"I don't think that at all," Olivia answered. "But you love working with children. You have a gift."

"You can't say that," Millie said stubbornly. "You barely know me. I could mess up that girl."

Olivia blew out a frustrated sigh. "I don't understand what happened at your internship last spring, but I know it's a shame you're giving up on your dreams."

"I'm not giving up," Millie argued. "I took a semester off school. Big deal."

"Hold on, ladies." Natalie held one hand out toward each of them. "Not that this demonstration of sibling dysfunction isn't fascinating, but let's get back to Jake." She pointed at Olivia. "From what little I know about him, I'm guessing he won't let anyone in the family help out. He always was a loner."

"He's only letting us assist with the bare essentials," Olivia agreed. "Sara's away at a movie premiere for a few days."

"Is it weird hanging out with a Hollywood star?" Millie couldn't help the question. She was oddly fascinated by the life her half sister had created for herself in Crimson. Olivia's friend Sara Wellens had been a popular child actor years ago and had recently had a resurgence in her career. She was also married to Jake's younger brother Josh, and together they ran a guest ranch outside of town.

Olivia smiled. "She's just Sara when she's in Crimson. You'll like her, Millie. She's got some of your spunk."

Millie couldn't imagine having anything in common with an A-list actress, but she didn't argue.

"Before she left," Olivia continued, "the two of us went over with groceries and meals for the freezer. We wanted to take Brooke out for the day, but she wouldn't leave Jake's side. Logan and Josh have been taking turns stopping by, but it's the same for them."

"Poor baby," Natalie murmured. "This has to be hard for her." She turned to Millie. "But Brooke liked *you*?"

Millie nodded. "Kids trust me. I think it's because I'm small. My mom is the same way—we put people at ease." She pushed her hair away from her face with one shoulder and took another cookie. "We're nonthreatening."

"Right," Olivia said with a harsh laugh. "Your mother was a threat to my family for decades. Joyce may be small, but she packs quite the emotional punch."

Millie didn't know how to respond to that. She and Olivia shared a father, a US Senator who'd remained married to Olivia's mother up until his death a few years ago. Married, but not faithful. Millie's mother, Joyce, had been Robert Palmer's mistress for almost thirty years. She'd built her life around being available to him whenever he needed her, never asking anything in return—no financial support, no pleas to leave his wife. Joyce was the perfect other woman, making the time Robert spent with them fun and easy—a break from the pressures of real life.

But it hadn't been a break for Millie. She'd needed more. She'd wanted a father who would come to school functions and swim-team meets. Hell, she would have been happy being able to tell her friends she *had* a father. But her mother had insisted they keep silent about Robert for the sake of his reputation and career. It had always been about him.

So, yes, she and her mom both had a gift for making people feel comfortable. Comfortable walking all over them. Millie didn't know how to do relationships any other way. That was why she gravitated toward children. Kids didn't keep secrets or have ulterior motives. And that was what had drawn her to Crimson, Colorado, and the half sister she hardly knew. Olivia had been kind to her, even though she had every reason to hate Millie. They were joined by a family history that had damaged them both.

"I'm not my mother." She hated that her chin trembled as she said the words.

"Thank heavens for that. But Jake is part of my family now." Olivia's voice was solemn. "Logan hardly sleeps at night for how bothered he is that Jake insists on doing everything himself. I asked you to do this because I trust you, Millie. Maybe I see something in you that you can't see in yourself right now, but it's there. I hope spending time in Crimson will enable you to discover it again." She smiled. "This place is special that way."

Emotion welled in Millie's chest. If Olivia believed she could help Jake Travers and his daughter, she wanted to prove her sister right. No one had ever put much stock in Millie. She'd been taught from a young age that the way to get ahead was to not make demands—to be amiable and fun and nothing more.

But Jake and Brooke needed more if they were going to make it as a family unit.

"You might be pushing it talking about Crimson being special," Natalie added, her expression doubtful. "My experience begs to differ."

Millie was certain Olivia's friend was trying to lighten the mood, for which Millie was grateful. "You're a Crimson native, right?"

"Born and raised." Natalie gave an exaggerated flip of her dark hair. "And only a little ashamed to admit it."

"You're still here," Olivia pointed out. "It's a wonderful place."

Natalie shrugged. "It has its good points. The Travers brothers are three of them." She turned to Millie. "So are you going to stay and help Jake, whether he wants it or not?"

This was it. Her chance to make a run for it. Millie knew Olivia would smooth things over with Jake as best she could. This entire situation had *train wreck* written all over it. She'd promised herself that she was going to start looking out for number one, but the instinct for self-preservation just wasn't in Millie's DNA.

She bit down on her lip until it hurt then nodded. "Although it's probably another on my long list of bad decisions, I'm going to stay."

Chapter Three

As soon as he heard Brooke's happy squeal, Jake knew Millie was back.

It had been almost two hours since she'd left to get her things from Olivia and Logan's, and the possibility that she wouldn't return had occurred to him only a couple thousand times.

He wouldn't have blamed her.

She might need a job, but his messed-up life was too complicated for most people to handle. Yes, his brothers and their wives had offered support more times than Jake could count since he'd returned to Crimson. But he was the oldest and the brother who'd never needed anything.

How could he admit to them that he was so weak?

All of their offers only brought back the flood of guilt about how he'd deserted their family years ago. He'd gotten a college scholarship that had enabled him to leave Crimson and their alcoholic father and never look back. Which he hadn't, even when his younger siblings needed him. Even when Logan's twin, Beth, had died in a tragic car accident. Even years later for their mother's funeral. Jake had used school, then his residency and his work to avoid the past.

He'd only returned because he had nowhere else to go. But he'd do all he could not to let himself depend on his brothers. He didn't deserve their kindness.

Still, they'd given it to him. Millie was proof of that. Jake would have gotten around to finding a nanny for Brooke, although even that had been difficult because he was too afraid of seeing pity in a stranger's eyes when they heard his story. Jake didn't want anyone's pity.

He lifted himself off the sofa, where he and Brooke had been watching some show about an oversize red dog in between her frequent trips to the window to watch for "Fairy Poppins," as she'd named Millie.

Millie had made it to the front door, a large roller suitcase at her feet and a duffel bag slung over her shoulder.

She met his gaze and blew out a breath. "You thought I was going to ditch you guys."

"I'm glad you're here," he answered, not bothering to deny his doubts. Years of being a surgeon had taught him to keep his emotions off his face, and it was disconcerting that she could read him so easily. "Let me take your bag."

"I can manage." Her eyes tracked to his right side for a moment.

"I'm not a total invalid, Millie." He reached out, plucked the bag from her shoulder and turned into the house.

He was pretty sure he heard her mutter, "Invalid, no. Idiot, maybe," but chose to ignore it.

"Want to see your room?" Brooke scooted past him, tugging Millie behind her.

He caught the faint scent of chocolate chip cookie, and his mind went immediately to his youngest brother.

Logan had been baking since he was a kid. In fact, Jake and Brooke had made their way quickly through a batch of Logan's oatmeal scotchies just last week.

"Me and Daddy cleaned it," Brooke continued.

"Impressive," Millie called over her shoulder.

"You haven't seen it yet," he answered and took the handle of her wheeled suitcase in his uninjured hand. He was glad Millie and Brooke had already disappeared toward the back of the house, since his progress was slow and not so steady as he balanced her luggage on his good side.

Eventually he made it to the back half of the house, where there was a bedroom, a bathroom and small sitting area. Sara had found this house for him to rent. He was grateful for her forethought in making sure it contained enough space for live-in help. Clearly she hadn't underestimated his postsurgical needs the way he had.

A bead of sweat trickled between his shoulder blades, another reminder of his weakness. Brooke popped out of the bedroom, beckoning him with a large swipe of her arm. "In here, Daddy."

Daddy.

She used the word so freely, although he'd done nothing to earn it. Of course, he knew how little that meant in the grand scheme of things. If the name *father* was given based on merit, Jake's dad would have had the title stripped from him decades before he'd died.

He poked his head in the room but didn't enter. Something about stepping into Millie Spencer's temporary bedroom felt as if it might mean more than he wanted it to.

"Does everything seem okay?" he asked, looking all around except where Millie was perched at the edge of the bed.

She stood quickly, her attention focused on brushing

the quilt smooth. Apparently he wasn't the only one affected by the unexpected intimacy of the moment.

"Perfect." Her voice squeaked just a little, making him smile. She glanced at her watch. "Do you have plans for dinner?"

"Pizza," Brooke yelled. "Can Fairy Poppins eat with us, Daddy?"

He saw Millie stifle a laugh. "You can call me Millie, Brooke."

"Millie Poppins?"

"Just Millie."

"What do you like on your pizza, Ms. Poppins?" he asked when Brooke's face fell.

"Don't you start now." Millie made a face. "And I'm fine with anything."

"Bacon and pepperoni," Brooke shouted.

"Inside voice," Millie told her.

Brooke crossed her arms over her chest. He hadn't known his daughter long, but already he could see a temper tantrum brewing. "She gets excited about pizza," he explained to Millie.

"Inside voice," she repeated, and suddenly he realized that Fairy Poppins had more backbone than he'd expected.

"We have pizza *a lot*," Brooke told Millie. Jake noticed that her decibel level had lowered a few notches. One point, Millie Spencer.

"Tomorrow we'll go to the grocery store." Millie ruffled Brooke's hair then turned to Jake. "Do you have peanut butter?"

"Um...yes."

Brooke shook her head. "Pizza and peanut butter don't go."

"It's for the gum in your hair," Millie told her. "We'll work on that after dinner."

"Mommy didn't let me have gum." Brooke stuck her fingers in her mouth, sucking hard.

"I bet you miss her very much," Millie said softly, bending to Brooke's level.

Brooke went totally still, but swiped the hand that wasn't occupied across her eyes.

Jake cleared his throat. "Millie's going to unpack now, Brooke. Would you help me order the pizza?"

She didn't move. Although it had happened only a couple of times since he'd picked her up from Stacy's parents, it scared the pants off Jake when she got like this. He knew what it was like to be paralyzed with emotion. "If you come with me, we'll get cinnamon sticks for dessert."

The promise of sugar broke the spell. She nodded and wiped her fingers on the front of her purple cotton dress. Without a word, she lifted her still-glistening hand to him. He swallowed and took it, once again dumbfounded that she trusted him so completely.

Millie stared at him, her hands clutched to her chest.

"We have a lot to talk about," he told her.

"Yes," she whispered, her lips barely moving.

"Pizza first," Brooke yelled, then repeated in a lower tone, "Pizza first."

"Pizza first," he agreed and led his daughter out of the room.

While Jake tucked Brooke in for bed later that night, Millie found a bottle of wine pushed to the back of the refrigerator and poured a tall glass. She wasn't a big drinker by nature but definitely needed some liquid fortification before talking to Jake Travers alone.

She took out a second glass as he came into the kitchen.

"I hope you don't mind that I helped myself," she said, turning to him.

"Knock yourself out," he answered.

If only it were that easy.

"Would you like a glass?"

He shook his head. "I take one pain pill a day when Brooke goes to bed. It doesn't mix well with alcohol."

"How much pain are you in?"

"It's not that bad," he said, not meeting her eyes. "It gets worse when I'm on my feet a lot or don't take time to rest."

"Which you don't, being a full-time father."

Stretching the splinted arm out in front of him, Jake curled his fingers a few times. "I have an appointment with the doctor tomorrow morning then physical therapy. I've had to cancel my last two appointments because Brooke wouldn't stay with anyone and I didn't want to take her with me."

"She's really bonded to you."

He looked at her now. The intensity in his gaze almost knocked her over. "It blows me away. I have no idea what I'm doing, and she doesn't care one bit."

"You're trying," Millie answered. "That counts for a lot."

His eyes narrowed, studying her. Millie realized she was doing exactly what her mother had always done. Smoothing things over, trying to make the man in front of her feel better even though she barely understood his situation. One of Millie's biggest weaknesses, inherited directly from her mother, was her habit of caring too quickly. She led with her emotions, and her first inclination was always to view people through rose-colored glasses.

For all she knew, Brooke would be better off with her grandparents. But Millie understood what it was like to have a father who only dropped in occasionally, always bearing toys or some other bribe for affection. Gifts couldn't make up for the long absences, to a little girl feeling alone and deserted by someone she wanted so desperately to love her.

Brooke had already lost one parent. Millie had to help Jake see that he could be a father, that an imperfect parent who was a solid part of his daughter's life was better than a fly-by-night dad.

She picked up the pad of paper and pen she'd found in one of the drawers and stepped forward to the kitchen table. "Let's make a list of what needs to be done, the schedule for you and Brooke, and where I fit into everything."

His blue eyes darkened and Millie suddenly had a clear picture of where she'd like to fit—pressed up against Jake's lean frame. He was more than a foot taller than she, so she could imagine how safe she'd feel tucked along his side. She didn't want to have this awareness of him—it felt new and unsettling, especially in the quiet of the evening. When Brooke was around, she was the focus of both their attention. Now Millie couldn't help but notice every detail about Jake, from the fullness of his mouth to the broad stretch of his shoulders underneath his faded T-shirt.

She also saw the tiny lines of exhaustion bracketing the edges of his eyes. That evidence of his fatigue brought her back to the present. She wasn't here because of her undeniable attraction to him as a man. Of course she had a reaction to him. Like Natalie said, all three of the Travers brothers were drop-dead gorgeous. Millie knew Olivia's husband, Logan, and had met the middle brother, Josh, on her first visit to Crimson. But there was something about Jake that drew her to him in a way she'd never experienced before.

More than anything that reaffirmed her commitment to keeping their relationship strictly professional.

"Money," she blurted.

He paused before lowering himself into the chair across from her. "Cutting right to the chase? I like it. We haven't discussed your salary."

"We should… I know you'll pay me…and I want to help you… I probably should have asked yesterday but…"

"One thousand."

"One thousand what?"

"Dollars. The majority of my rehabilitation will take place in the first month and a half, according to the doctors. By then, I'll know if the nerve damage has healed enough for me to do surgery again. Brooke's grandparents are coming out in two weeks, but I still want you full-time through the duration of my stay in Crimson."

"One thousand dollars for six weeks of work?" Millie hadn't made much working in preschools over the past couple of years, but her ability to live on a tight budget only went so far.

One side of his mouth quirked. "I'll pay you one thousand dollars a week for six weeks. You're staying at the house, so it's like you're on twenty-four-hour call. You'll have no rent, and I'll buy all the groceries."

She felt her eyes widen. "I can't accept so much money."

"I don't think that's the right response," he said with a laugh. "And I can't cook. I buy the groceries, but you're in charge of meals." He patted his flat stomach. "I can't handle another night of take-out pizza."

"You're a terrible negotiator," Millie said. "No one starts with their best offer."

His smile widened. "How do you know that's my best offer?"

"Are you some sort of secret billionaire who can throw money around like it's nothing?"

"I have plenty of savings and a great disability policy." He leaned forward, the tips of his fingers brushing the back of her hand. "I believe you get what you pay for, and you're worth what I'm offering."

He was touching one tiny patch of her skin, but she felt the reverberation of it through her entire body. Before tonight, no one had ever thought she was worth much. She'd taken jobs in preschools and day-care centers because she liked being around kids. It had taken her years to believe she might actually have some talent for teaching. But when she'd tried to make a career of that, she'd made a mess of her college internship.

Millie knew she needed this job as much as Jake needed her. Not for the money, but because her self-confidence had been torn to shreds. She wanted to prove that she could make a difference.

For someone.

For this man.

"You won't regret it," she said softly, tapping her pen against the pad of paper. "Now let's start that list."

Chapter Four

Jake jerked awake, pushing the covers aside as he scrambled from the bed. His heart raced as memories of the earth shaking while the hotel collapsed around him assaulted his mind. The intense pain that shot through his leg when he tried to put weight on his right foot brought him back to reality. He sank to the edge of the bed, bending forward with his hands on his knees, and took several breaths to clear his head.

Reliving those last moments of the aftershock had become a recurring nightmare. He and Stacy Smith, Millie's mother, had never been in love—theirs was a relationship born from close proximity and convenience. But he'd cared about her and still couldn't accept that he hadn't been able to save her. Now a little girl—his daughter—was motherless.

For the hundredth time, he wished it would have been him instead. Sure, his brothers would have mourned him, but there was no one who needed him the way Brooke needed her mother. His daughter had been sad but accepting of her loss, a fact that only made Jake want to change the past even more, as impossible as that was. He was trying his best to honor Stacy's request that he form a relationship with Brooke even though he continued to feel out of his element at every turn.

He glanced at the clock, then toward the window at the light peeking through the edge of the curtain. Normally his dreams woke him in the predawn hours and he'd lie awake with his guilt and panic until Brooke came in to start the morning. But if it was really close to eight, he'd slept over an hour longer than normal. Hoisting himself onto his feet, he grabbed a T-shirt from the dresser and made his way to the kitchen.

"Daddy!" Brooke called when she spotted him in the doorway that separated the back hall from the family room and kitchen. His heart twisted as she ran across the room, a plastic tiara askew on her head despite the fact that she still wore her polka-dot pajamas.

She grabbed his hand and tugged him through the family room, which was now shockingly clean compared to how it had looked the previous night.

"Me and Fairy Poppins cleaned," Brooke said as if she could read his mind.

"Millie," a voice called from behind the pantry door. "You know my name is Millie, Brookie-Cookie."

His daughter dissolved into a fit of giggles as Millie shut the pantry. This morning his new nanny looked less like a woodland sprite and more like a woodcutter's fantasy come to life. She wore faded cargo shorts and a soft flannel shirt over a cream-colored tank top. Her chin-length hair was pulled back from her face with a wide headband, showing her delicate features to full advantage. Although she was tiny, the cut of the shorts made her legs look long and trim, and Jake had to shut his eyes to stop his gaze from roaming her body.

"We made pancakes," Brooke told him. "The real kind from homemade."

"Homemade pancakes?" He crouched down to her eye level. "They smell delicious, sweetie. Thank you for making breakfast."

"Thank Fairy—I mean Millie—too."

He straightened again and turned to Millie, who was pouring juice into three glasses. "I didn't even know we had the ingredients to make pancakes."

She nodded but didn't look at him. "The cupboards and refrigerator are well stocked. I was a little surprised, to tell you the truth."

"Olivia and Sara keep the groceries coming. I haven't even used half the stuff they've brought."

"That makes sense."

He watched her set the juice on the kitchen table. Up until this point, all he'd managed was bagels and cereal for breakfast. "Thank you, Millie."

"It's my job," she answered, and for some reason those three words annoyed the hell out of him. "Do you want coffee?"

"I'll get it." He moved toward the counter at the same time she turned from the table. She ran straight into him then stumbled. Despite the pain that shot through his leg, he reached out to steady her, keeping his fingers on her arms until she looked up at him. "Thank you for breakfast."

"You're welcome," she said, her voice breathless in a way that made him think she wasn't totally immune to him.

Strange how gratifying that felt.

"I'll pour the coffee." Reluctantly, he released his hold on her. "You ladies sit down and start."

He joined them a minute later as Millie was spooning fresh fruit onto each of the plates.

"Daddy, will you cut my pancakes?" Brooke asked, sliding her plate toward him.

"I can do it," Millie said, reaching over the table.

"I want Daddy to cut them."

"You bet." He didn't look at Millie as he picked up a knife in his right hand. It was awkward with the wrist brace. The truth was he hadn't cut a damn thing, even food, since before the accident. He forced his stiff fingers to grip the knife and slowly sliced the two pancakes, embarrassed that a trickle of sweat had curled down his back by the time he was finished. "How about syrup?" he asked when he'd finished, making his voice casual.

"Lots!" Brooke bounced up and down in her seat.

He poured the syrup, then set the plate down in front of his daughter.

"Yum," she said around the first mouthful.

"How often do you have physical therapy?"

He quickly put down the knife as he met Millie's gaze. Was it that obvious how much difficulty he was having?

"I'm scheduled for three days a week." He used his fork to carve off a bite of pancakes from his own stack. "I've missed a couple of sessions, though, so I've been doing the exercises at home."

"I don't like Daddy to leave me," Brooke announced matter-of-factly.

"Your daddy has to go to his appointments so he can get better. We'll have lots of fun together until he's done."

"Can I have my screen time then?"

He glanced at Millie. "What's screen time?"

"You know, the amount of time Brooke has each day to watch television or play games on the computer."

"Like PBS Kids," Brooke clarified for him. "You know, when I play 'Curious George.'"

"I thought that was educational." He stabbed a few more pancake pieces onto his fork. "Isn't educational a good thing?"

Millie gave him a gentle smile—a teacher smile, he thought with a spark of irritation. The kind that reminded him that he didn't know what he was doing as a parent.

"Educational television *is* good, but..."

"Not like the zombies," Brooke interrupted. She scrunched her face up at the memory.

Millie's eyes widened a fraction. "Zombies?"

Jake blew out a breath. "A commercial for some TV show came on while I was watching SportsCenter. It was graphic... I turned it off as soon as I realized."

"It gave me nightmares." Brooke licked a bit of syrup off the tip of one finger. "Like Daddy has when he thinks of Mommy."

He heard Millie suck in a breath but kept his eyes focused on the table, unable to form a coherent response to his daughter's observation.

"My dreams about Mommy are nice," she continued. "I have a good one about when she took me to the zoo and we saw a baby orangutan. I'm going to give Daddy some of my dreams at night. Then we can both sleep better."

Now he did look at his daughter, unable to keep his eyes off her. "Thank you, sweetheart. I want you to keep those good dreams for yourself." It was difficult to speak past the ball of emotion knotting at the base of his throat.

"I have plenty." Brooke smiled at him then turned her attention to her plate, using her fork to make designs in the leftover syrup.

He heard a tiny whimper and glanced over at Millie, who quickly wiped at the corners of her eyes with a napkin. "How about if we save your screen time for tonight, Brooke? Let's rent a movie to watch after dinner. We need to drop your daddy off at his appointment and then we'll go to the park. Maybe pack a picnic lunch?"

Brooke nodded. "I like mac 'n cheese for lunch."

"Got it." She stood and cleared most of the dishes from the table.

Jake followed her to the sink. "Is it any wonder," he whispered, "that I let her have as much 'screen time' as she wants? Without the TV or computer as a distraction, she'd be slaying me with her innocent comments all day long." He put down his plate and gripped the edge of the counter. "I'm in over my head here, Millie. It's not a sensation I'm used to, and I don't know how to handle it."

"You'll be fine. This is new for both of you. Brooke went through a huge loss. The most important thing is that you're here for her. She *needs* you, Jake."

He wasn't sure if he could handle being needed, if he had the strength to make it work. But that wasn't a conversation for right now. Brooke's unconditional love coupled with Millie's expectations of him doing the right thing crippled him almost as much as his injuries. His motto during emergency missions had always been Stay in the Moment. He could only deal with one thing at a time and right now that was getting caught up on his physical therapy. He was in no position to make any decisions about the future until he knew what his body would be able to handle.

"Thanks for breakfast," he told Millie before turning away.

Her hand on his bare arm stopped him. Her touch was

cool and soft against his skin. "You'll be fine, Jake," she repeated. "We're going to make sure of it."

He gave a tense nod then walked to the kitchen table, reaching down to straighten Brooke's tiara. "Best pancakes ever."

Her smile was bright. "Millie's going to teach me how to make Frenchy toast tomorrow."

"I can't wait." He unstuck a strand of hair from her cheek. "I'm going to get cleaned up for my appointment. Wash your face and hands and we'll pick out an outfit for today."

She shook her head. "Millie will help me get dressed." She grinned. "She's a girl, Daddy, so she's better at clothes than you."

He'd wager Millie was better with everything relating to kids than he, but he didn't point out that fact.

"Sounds like a plan, Stan."

"Daddy." She giggled. "You know my name's not Stan."

He thumped the heel of his palm against his forehead. "I keep forgetting. It's a plan, *Brooke*."

"Silly Daddy. That's better."

One tiny thing was better. He only wished he could fix the rest of their problems so easily.

By the time she got the dishwasher loaded, the table wiped down and Brooke cleaned and dressed for the day, Millie had almost gotten her emotions under control.

Almost.

There was no doubt that Millie had gone through hell as a child, never able to claim her father publicly or even tell anyone she knew the man who'd helped create her. Her visits with Robert Palmer had been behind closed doors or incognito. She'd hated all the pretending she'd had to do. Hated that when her father was around, her mother insisted that Millie not trouble him. There had been no help with homework, no demands for more of his time or requests to attend a school performance. But she'd known him. He'd been a presence—albeit an occasional one—in her life.

Brooke had lost her mother, and at four, Millie knew the girl couldn't truly understand the permanence of the situation or what it meant for someone to be dead. It was trauma at a level Millie could hardly comprehend. Yet Brooke seemed to be handling it with a mix of cheerfulness and poignant honesty that touched Millie to her core.

She smiled as Brooke played with her hair while Millie strapped the girl into her car seat. It was a tight fit in the back of her VW Beetle, not a car she'd planned on using to haul around a child and her very tall father. She focused on the task at hand and tried to ignore the fact that her back end was on full display as she adjusted the child safety straps to make Brooke more comfortable.

Readjusting her headband, she turned then narrowed her eyes at the smug smile playing at the corner of Jake's mouth.

"I'm not thinking what you think I am," he said softly, his blue eyes appearing several shades darker than she remembered. "Promise."

"Toss me Bunny." She held out her hands, willing her body to stop responding to the wicked gleam in his eye.

Instead he took the few steps toward her until they stood toe to toe. He placed the stuffed animal in her arms then traced his finger from the corner of her jaw down her neck, straightening the collar of her flannel shirt in the process. "You're blushing."

"I'm just hot."

"You're *just* hot," he repeated.

"Not like that. You know what I mean. It was a lot

of work maneuvering that car seat into the back of the Beetle."

He gave a small laugh. "Right now I'm wondering how I'm going to maneuver *myself* into your car."

"It's not that small. You'll fit fine." When he flashed a wide grin, she groaned but couldn't stop herself from smiling in response. Something about Jake put her at ease enough to enjoy the playful banter. "Get your mind out of the gutter, Dr. Travers." She turned and handed Brooke the stuffed animal then went around the car to slip in behind the wheel.

She tried not to watch as Jake attempted to fold himself into the passenger seat. "How tall are you, Millie?"

"Five feet, two and a half inches."

He gave her a look out of the corner of his eye.

"In half-inch heels," she amended. "You're what, six-three?"

"And a quarter." He adjusted the seat back then lifted his booted leg into the car and shut the door. "If an extra quarter inch matters to you."

"Daddy, you're smushing me," Brooke said, and Millie saw the girl kick her foot into the back of Jake's seat.

He moved the seat up again, his knees grazing the dash. "Is that better?"

"Uh-huh. Bunny needs room to spread out."

"Lucky Bunny," Jake mumbled.

Millie looked over, ready to continue their verbal sparring until she noticed the tight set of his mouth. Jake's head was resting back against the seat, his eyes closed.

She placed her hand on his arm. "Are you okay?"

He gave a small nod but didn't open his eyes. "Just not used to this much moving around so early in the day. Sad but true."

"It will get better." She realized she'd said a version

of that phrase almost a dozen times in the past twenty-four hours. Speaking the words out loud, unfortunately, didn't make them reality.

She backed the car out of the driveway and followed Jake's directions to the hospital. When she'd visited Olivia before in Crimson, there had still been snow on the ground. Now the whole valley had come to life and the mountains rising up from the outskirts of town were a mix of the dark green of pine trees and the lighter shades of aspens. Even Brooke seemed awed by their surroundings, as she was quiet for most of the drive.

She pulled into the hospital's parking lot fifteen minutes later.

"You can drop me off at the main entrance," Jake said before she could ask the question.

"No!" Brooke suddenly shouted from the backseat. "Daddy, don't go. Don't go to the hospital."

Jake turned as best he could toward the back of the car. "We talked about this, Brooke. I have an appointment and then I'll be with you again. Millie's going to take care of you until then."

"No," Brooke said again. This time Millie could hear the tears in the young girl's voice. "You can't leave me."

Millie's heart ached at those words. Jake met her gaze. "What do I do?"

"Brookie-Cookie," Millie said over the girl's sniffling, "we'll walk your daddy into the hospital." She parked the car in a space as close to the front of the hospital as she could find. "You can see where they're going to do the physical therapy and the office where his doctor works. If you want, we can stay and wait for him."

"Okay." Brooke's voice was a tiny whimper.

Millie could see a muscle tick in Jake's jaw but ignored him as she unstrapped Brooke from her car seat and helped her out of the car. Brooke took her father's hand as they walked toward the sliding doors at the front of the building. She sang a song to Bunny as she skipped along, once again content since she wasn't being separated from her father.

Millie came to Jake's other side. "She's afraid of losing you if you're out of her sight for too long," she whispered.

"I could be here for a couple of hours." He glanced at her. "Do you really want to hang out here all morning?"

"I'm hoping that if she sees the office and maybe meets some people, that will make her feel better and we can leave." She shrugged. "If not, we'll stay." She made her smile bright. "You're paying me a lot of money to take care of your daughter. I'll make it work, Jake."

He led them to the elevators and, once they reached the third floor, down the hall to the rehabilitation and physical-therapy offices. He walked forward, Brooke still glued to his side, to check in at the reception desk.

"I have a nine-thirty appointment," he told the woman behind the counter.

Millie watched as the woman glanced up then did a double take. She could imagine Jake got that reaction quite a bit, although he didn't seem to notice. "Oh, my goodness," the woman gushed, "it's really you."

Jake's expression remained blank.

"Don't you remember me?" The woman smiled. "I'm Lauren Bell. We went to high school together. You missed the five-, ten- and fifteen-year reunions, Jake. And you were our valedictorian." She tsked softly. "Of course, I see your brothers around town but never hear anything about you. I know you became a doctor and you travel all around the world. It must be so exciting."

Jake glanced at Millie with a look that screamed for help. She shook her head.

"It's…um… Yes, I'm a surgeon." He held up his arm. "I was a surgeon."

"Well, we'll take good care of you." Her smile faltered as Brooke stood on her tiptoes to see over the counter. "I didn't know you had a child."

"Me neith—"

Millie coughed.

"This is my daughter, Brooke."

Brooke waved and lifted her stuffed animal in the air. "This is Bunny."

"And your wife?" Lauren asked with a curious glance toward Millie.

"I'm not married," Jake explained. "Millie is Brooke's nanny while we're in town."

The predatory gleam that flamed in Lauren Bell's eyes had Millie clenching her hands. "A bunch of us from the old group get together for happy hour at the Two Moon Saloon on Fridays after work. You should join us sometime. If the nanny does evenings."

"The old group," Jake repeated slowly. "Yeah, sure, I'll see what I can do."

Brooke tugged on his hand. "You won't leave me, right?"

Millie saw him close his eyes for a moment. When he opened them, he gave a sweet and sexy—damn him—smile to Lauren Bell. "Since we're friends, Lauren," he said, leaning forward as if he were sharing a secret, "do you think it would be okay if Brooke had a little tour of the offices before I got started? Maybe you could introduce us to some of the therapists and she could see what I'm going to be doing while I'm here." He winked. Millie suppressed a gag. "She's kind of nervous and I'm sure you know all the ins and outs of how things work around here."

Lauren stood and called over her shoulder, “Rhonda, watch the front desk for a few minutes.” She turned back to Jake. “Does the nanny need to come with us?”

He shook his head without looking at Millie. “Just you, me and Brooke.”

Millie was surprised Lauren didn’t do a fist pump in the air.

“I’ll take you back. Come through that door to the left of the waiting room and I’ll meet you there.”

Jake led Brooke past Millie. “Good start, right?”

She rolled her eyes. “For someone who has no charm, you really laid it on thick just now.”

“Who said I had no charm?”

“Personal observation.”

“I’ve got loads of charm, Fairy Poppins.” He wiggled his eyebrows. “But only a lucky few are on the receiving end of it.”

Millie coughed out a laugh. Without taking her eyes off Jake she said, “Your ‘old friend’ is dousing herself with body mist at the moment. Be careful how you wield that charm, Dr. Travers. It’s quite a weapon.”

He gave a mock shudder. “Let’s go, Brooke, and whatever you do, don’t let go of my hand.”

She saw Brooke squeeze his fingers tighter. “Be back soon, Millie,” the girl said, clutching Bunny to her chest.

Ten minutes later, the door to the waiting room opened again. Millie tossed aside the magazine she’d been pretending to read as Brooke skipped through the door, followed by her father.

“Look, look,” Brooke squealed, running forward to Millie. “I got a stressy ball, and a pen and notepad with the phone number here on it.” She thrust the notepad forward. “So if we need to call Daddy when he’s here, we can.”

“We don’t need to stay?”

Brooke shook her head. "Daddy's going to text me pictures to your phone so I can keep track of him. And we'll get lunch ready because he's going to be really hungry after his therapy stuff."

Millie stood as Jake walked up. She could see a woman in a polo shirt and khaki pants waiting just inside the reception door for him. "Everything's good?"

He nodded. "Your idea worked." He ruffled Brooke's hair. "Now that Bunny has seen everything that happens at the office, he feels much better about me being here." His gaze was warm on Millie, making parts of her body tingle that had no business coming to life for Jake Travers. "Thank you," he said softly.

Before she could reply, Brooke held up the stuffed animal. "Give Bunny a kiss goodbye, Daddy."

Jake's mouth dropped open an inch. "How about a high five?"

Her mouth set in a stubborn way that made Millie think of Jake. Already like father, like daughter. "A kiss."

He bent forward and touched his lips to the animal's grungy fur.

"Me, too," Brooke said, angling her cheek toward him.

He glanced up at Millie, emotion clouding his eyes. She nodded, the tingling in her body rapidly progressing to a full-on tremble.

Jake kissed his daughter's cheek then the top of her head. Millie wasn't sure if the sigh she heard came from her or the therapist waiting for him. Jake straightened and she noticed a faint color across his cheeks. The doctor was actually blushing. Why was vulnerability so darned appealing when it came wrapped up in an alpha-male package?

He glanced at the clock on the wall then met her gaze, looking embarrassed and flustered. "I'm going to meet with one of the orthopedic surgeons on staff after this. Give me a few hours and I'll be ready to go."

"Remember the pictures, Daddy."

"I will, Brooke. You ladies have fun."

He walked away but looked over his shoulder before the waiting-room door closed behind him. "Thanks again, Millie. For everything this morning."

She lifted her hand, trying for a casual wave but feeling pretty sure she looked more like she was having an uncontrollable body spasm. "Just doing my job," she called out brightly.

His eyes clouded a bit at her words and she immediately regretted them. But before she could say anything else, he was gone.

Chapter Five

After struggling to get Brooke back into her car seat, Millie left a message for her sister. She needed to do something about her car situation if she was going to be driving Jake and Brooke all over Crimson.

While she waited to hear back, she and Brooke went to the grocery and then stopped at the bakery she'd seen on her way through town. The main street through downtown was bustling with people on this gorgeous late-summer day. She knew that tourism was big business in Crimson. Olivia had been married to the town's former mayor before she divorced him and met Jake's brother Logan. Now she managed the community center that offered programs for both locals and nonresidents. The popular gift shop attached to the center sold goods from local artists. Jake's other brother, Josh, owned and operated a guest ranch on the outskirts of town along with his Hollywood-actress wife, Sara.

The town was picture-postcard cute, and she could understand why tourists would find this town irresistible. Colorful Victorian buildings lined the street, and the majestic peaks of the Rocky Mountains served as a backdrop. Crimson embodied a kind of small-town charm and friendliness she guessed might be lacking in tonier mountain resorts.

"What's your favorite kind of muffin?" she asked Brooke as they made their way to the Life Is Sweet bakery.

"Blueberry," Brooke answered without hesitation.

"Yum. Mine, too." Millie tipped her sunglasses back on her head. "I bet they have blueberry."

"We need Frenchy toast bread," Brooke added, tossing her rabbit into the air.

"And bread for French toast," Millie agreed. *Plus a giant vanilla latte*, she thought to herself.

The moment she opened the door to the bakery, the smell of sugar, bread and roasting coffee filled the air. She took a deep breath and led Brooke toward the counter. The interior was adorable, with pale yellow walls and lights strung across the ceiling. The counter was made of wood planks, and the same warm trim was at the base on the walls and around the door frames.

A large chalkboard menu filled the back wall of the room and the glass display was filled with scrumptious-looking cakes, muffins, cookies and pastries. A cluster of tables sat to one side of the room, and a few customers were clearly enjoying their selections.

Brooke let out a rapturous sigh. "I love it here," she whispered.

Millie smiled. "Me, too, Cookie." She spotted Natalie Holt at a table near the front of the store and waved.

"Hey, girl." Natalie motioned Millie and Brooke to

join her. She sat with another woman, who smiled as they approached. "How's the first day with the hot doc going?"

Millie made a face. "This is Jake's daughter, Brooke," she told Natalie.

"Oops." Natalie smiled, not looking embarrassed at all. "Nice to meet you, sweet pea."

Brooke grabbed hold of Millie's shirt but smiled at Natalie. "Millie calls me Cookie." Brooke held out her stuffed rabbit. "You can too if you want. This is Bunny. My mommy gave him to me for my birthday. She's dead now."

Natalie's smile turned gentle. She reached out a hand to gently pet the stuffed animal. "I bet having Bunny with you helps you remember your mommy."

Brooke nodded then looked up at Millie. "Can I have a blueberry muffin now?"

"You're in luck." Natalie pointed to the woman across from her, who was dabbing at her eyes. Millie understood the effect Brooke could have with her candid innocence. "This is Ms. Katie and she owns the bakery."

The woman, who looked young for a business owner, stood and held out her hand to Millie. "I'm Katie Garrity. It's nice to meet you. I'm also a friend of your sister's."

Millie took her hand. "Olivia's made a good life in Crimson," she said, trying not to sound jealous of her sister's perfect life filled with friends in a community she loved. Trying not to *feel* jealous.

"She's a wonderful part of our community." She bent down in front of Brooke. "Did I hear you say you'd like a blueberry muffin?"

"They're my favorite."

"I just happen to know that fresh blueberry muffins came out of the oven a little while ago. They should be cooled by now. Would you like to come to the kitchen? We'll wrap one up for you."

Brooke bounced on her toes. "Can I go, Millie?"

"As long as you listen to Ms. Katie when you're with her." Millie held out her hand. "How about if I hold Bunny until you get back?"

"He wants to go with me." Her big blue eyes met Millie's again. "You won't leave me, right?"

"I'll be right here."

"What would you like, Millie?"

"A vanilla latte if it's not too much trouble."

Katie's smile was as sweet as the scent of her pastries. "No trouble at all."

"Fairy Poppins likes blueberry muffins, too," Brooke announced.

Millie heard Natalie choke back a laugh. Katie's grin widened.

"You know that's not my name," Millie told Brooke.

"It's the name Daddy calls you."

"Daddy and I are going to have a talk later," Millie said, blowing out a breath.

Katie put a gentle hand on Brooke's back. "Let's see about those muffins."

They disappeared into the back of the bakery as Millie sank into the chair across from Natalie. "This is way more complicated than I expected."

"Second thoughts?" Natalie asked.

Millie shook her head. "No, but I wish I knew how to help more." She pointed to Natalie. "You handled Brooke's comment about her mother better than I did the first time she made one to me."

"I work at a retirement home, sometimes in the Alzheimer's unit." Natalie shrugged. "I deal with a lot of honesty and a lot of death. Kids are different than seniors, but people need to talk about the ones they've lost. It doesn't help to pretend like everything's normal when it isn't."

"You're right. I know that. I took a college class on children and grief, but it's different when the situation is real."

"Where's Jake today?"

"He's at the hospital. He had a physical-therapy appointment and was meeting with a doctor after."

"From what Olivia and Sara have told me, it's a good sign that Brooke was willing to stay with you."

"I think so. There's just so much to do. Brooke needs a normal schedule. Jake needs time to process everything that's happened. She takes all of his attention when they're together."

"What about preschool?"

"I don't know if Jake will go for that. He's already paying me more than he should to be the nanny. I could certainly teach her whatever a preschool could."

"But you can't get her the socialization with children her own age. I'm sure she had activities before everything changed." Natalie pulled her purse off the empty chair next to her. "There's a fantastic preschool here in town, Crimson Community Preschool. Most of us just call it CCP. My son went there and loved every minute of it."

"Do you only have one child?"

Natalie nodded. "I'm raising Austin on my own, so one is plenty. He's eight now. It's been just the two of us for as long as he can remember."

"That must be difficult. A single mother raised me, so I have an idea of how much work it can be. Do you have family in town?"

Natalie shook her head. "My mom is here but busy

with her own life. Austin and I are a good team. My friends support me, and the people I work with are great."

"Have you lived in Crimson your whole life? You never left, even for college or—"

"I never saw any reason to leave," Natalie said quickly, and Millie got the impression she didn't want to talk about her life in Crimson any further. That was fine. Millie knew all about keeping things to herself.

Natalie took out a pen and notepad from her purse and copied a number from her phone onto the paper. "Here's the preschool's number. Talk to Laura Wilkes, the director. Tell her you're a friend of mine."

Millie took the paper. "Thank you."

"You *do* have friends here," Natalie said as she stood. "Crimson is a great place, Millie. You should think about sticking around for good. It would make Olivia happy and I think you'd like it here."

"I don't..." Millie tapped her fingers against the table. She almost couldn't imagine being part of a community like Crimson. It was too good to be true. "I'll think about it."

Katie and Brooke reappeared from the kitchen just then. Katie balanced two plates in one hand and held a travel cup of coffee in the other. Brooke grasped a large brown paper bag under one arm.

"I've got to get back to work," Natalie called. "Thanks for the coffee break, Katie."

"Anytime," Katie said as she approached the table. "Drop Austin off whenever works best tonight. I'm excited to hang out with him."

"You're the best." With a wave to Brooke, Natalie headed out of the bakery.

Katie set the coffee cup and plates down on the table and took a seat near Millie. "Brooke told me you also needed bread for French toast. I gave you a loaf of brioche that will be perfect."

"Thanks," Millie said and took a long drink of coffee. "This is perfect."

Her phone beeped and she glanced down at it. "Your daddy sent you a picture, Brookie-Cookie." She held out the phone so Brooke could see the photo of Jake waving with his good hand while his other one was stretched out on a table as he squeezed a small ball. "He's doing exercises to make his hand stronger."

"I used to do exercises at tumbling class." Brooke put the bag on an empty chair, Bunny perched on top. "Ms. Katie has a mixer this big," she told Millie, arms outstretched. "And so much sugar for making things sweet."

"Like these muffins." Millie patted the seat next to her. "Climb up here and let's eat." She took her wallet from her purse and looked at Katie. "How much do I owe you for all of this?"

"It's on the house," Katie answered easily. "A 'welcome to Crimson' gift."

"You don't have to do that." Millie pulled out a twenty-dollar bill and tried to hand the money to Katie.

The other woman waved it away. "I want to. It's a nice thing you're doing, helping out Jake."

"He's paying me," Millie protested.

Katie smiled. "I know all the Travers brothers, although I was closest in age to Josh growing up. It's going to be hard for Jake being back in town like this. He was a bit of a loner growing up and so darn smart."

"He's got a lot to deal with, but he's doing okay." Millie found it odd that she felt the need to defend him to someone who probably understood a lot more about the situation than she did.

Katie leaned over to look at the photo on Millie's

phone. "Talk about getting better with age," she said then gave a low whistle. "It's been years since I've seen Jake, but he never fails to impress. You know everyone in the family has been so worried about him. They've managed to keep what happened under wraps, but that can only last so long in a town this size."

"The woman working the front desk at the physical-therapy office recognized him. I guess they went to high school together. Her name was Lauren."

"Lauren Bell?" Katie scrunched up her nose. "She should have the details of his return posted on Facebook within hours."

"Isn't that a HIPAA violation?"

"Not those details. I mean about Jake—what he looks like now, details about his daughter—"

"The fact that a hot, single doctor has returned to town is big news, huh?"

"In certain circles."

One of the young guys working behind the counter called out to Katie and she stood. "I've got to get back to work," she told Millie. "After Labor Day things will slow down around here. Maybe we can get together for a hike?"

"A hike?"

Katie laughed. "You know, walking on a trail in the woods. Quite popular in Colorado."

"Right." Millie knew what a hike was; she just couldn't believe Katie Garrity was inviting her on one. Growing up, Millie and her mom had kept to themselves. Her mother thought it made things easier when Millie's father came around—they could be available at a moment's notice and there weren't questions from curious friends about Millie's dad or lack of one.

It was a habit that had stuck, the inability to form

lasting friendships. It was part of what had kept Millie moving from place to place once she'd left home. But something about this quaint mountain town already lulled her into a strange sense of belonging. She wondered if it was time to explore that more.

"I grew up in the city," she told Katie. "I don't have a lot of experience with nature-ish stuff. But I'd like to hike with you."

"Then I'm guessing you've never fly-fished."

"I've never any kind of fished."

Katie's eyes took on an excited gleam. "Add that to your list, Millie. I'm going to make it my personal mission to turn you into a mountain girl."

"Me, too!" Brooke said, taking another big bite of muffin. "I can be a mountain-girl princess."

"We need more of those around here," Katie agreed. "I'll see you two soon, I hope."

Millie couldn't help her smile as Katie walked away. She was already half in love with the town of Crimson, Colorado.

Jake was already counting the days until he could escape his hometown. There was a reason he hadn't returned to Crimson for so many years. He liked privacy, the unfamiliar and starting new adventures. Coming back to Crimson was like trying to fit into a pair of shoes he'd grown out of a long time ago. It felt uncomfortable and cramped.

Maybe his mood had more to do with the past couple of hours. According to both the physical therapist and the orthopedic surgeon he'd seen, his wrist was healing on schedule. But there was still a question as to whether he'd ever regain full range of motion in his fingers or if the intermittent numbness in his hand would stop. He'd received several messages from the director of the agency he worked for over the past week, wanting an update and to make plans for the future.

How could Jake make any decisions without knowing if the career he'd worked so hard for was finished?

He stepped out into the bright light of a beautiful Colorado day, unable to appreciate the bluebird sky or pine-scented breeze that greeted him. He scanned the parking lot for Millie's yellow Beetle, then saw her waving from the side of a Ford Explorer. As he got closer, Jake noticed the writing on the side of the SUV that read Crimson Ranch, the name of the guest ranch his brother owned outside of town.

"Where'd you get this thing?" he asked, not bothering to hide the irritation in his voice.

Millie shrugged. "I saw it idling at the curb downtown with the keys in the ignition, so I took it."

"Smart aleck." He shook his head, but felt the ghost of a smile curl one side of his mouth. "This is one of Josh's vehicles."

"Glad you noticed," she said sweetly.

"Where's your car?"

"At the ranch." She tossed a set of keys in the air and caught them. "I made a trade."

"What use does Josh have for a VW Beetle?"

"He doesn't, but we need a car with more room."

"I don't need help from my brother. Your car was fine."

She patted the hood of the Explorer. "Well, I think a big rig kind of suits me."

He choked out a laugh at that. He heard a muffled shout from the back of the Explorer.

"As much fun as it is to argue about something so meaningless, you might want to greet your daughter. I didn't want her running through the parking lot, but she's beside herself with excitement to see you."

He took a deep breath, hoping to ease a little of the tension that had built around his shoulders. He stepped forward and opened the SUV's back door. "Hey there, Brooke." Thanks to the extra height of the Explorer, he was able to lean in and ruffle his daughter's hair without a problem.

"Daddy, you're back. You didn't die in the hospital."

Jake's mouth went dry. "I'm just fine, princess. My appointments were great and the doc says I'll be able to get rid of the boot and my wrist splint in a few weeks."

Brooke gave him a smile that almost cracked his heart in two. "I'm glad you didn't die, Daddy." Before he could answer, she continued, "Millie and I had so much fun. We went to the playground and the bakery with a ginormo mixer. I had a blueberry muffin and so did she, but I didn't finish mine, so she ate them both. We bought lots of healthy stuff at the grocery and some food you like, too. Then we made sandwiches and we're going to have a picnic with a blanket and lemonade. And I got a bug catcher at the grocery for grasshoppers and ladybugs and stuff."

"Sounds like your morning was more fun than mine."

"It was the best," she confirmed.

He knew he shouldn't care that the best morning his daughter had spent since they'd arrived in Crimson didn't involve him, but it was a difficult fact to ignore. "I'm ready for that picnic," he said and closed her door before climbing into the front passenger side.

"She missed you," Millie said softly as she shifted the car into Drive.

"While having the best day ever," he answered, aware that he sounded like a petulant schoolboy.

"I mean it, Jake. Brooke talked about you all morning long and she loved getting the photos you texted."

She pulled out onto the county road in front of the hospital, back toward town. He wanted to give her a phone book to sit on while she drove since she looked so small in the Explorer compared to how she'd fit in her tiny Beetle. Jake, on the other hand, relished the additional space to stretch out his leg.

"Did you see Josh when you picked this up?"

She shook her head. "Josh was taking a group out on an ATV tour. Sara was there with her friend April. We're going to dinner at the ranch tonight. Logan and Olivia are coming, too."

"No."

She glanced over at him, "Why? Are you too tired? We can go home now so you can rest."

"I'm not too tired." He scrubbed his hand across his face. "I'm used to going days without sleep, operating for hours at a time. One morning of physical therapy isn't going to wear me out." Which wasn't exactly true, but his pride wouldn't allow him to admit as much.

"Do you have other plans?" Her voice took on a vaguely suspicious tone. "Maybe with your *old friend* Lauren?"

"I don't want to have dinner with my brothers. It's as simple as that."

She shook her head. "That's not simple at all. They care about you, Jake. They want to know everything's okay."

"Everything's not okay, Millie." He squeezed shut his eyes. "I'm a shell of who I was before the accident. I don't want them fawning all over me, trying to make things better."

"They love you," she said gently. "They're your family. Why did you come back here if you don't want to see them?"

"I didn't know where else to go."

He saw her glance at him out of the corner of her eye and turned his head toward the window. Colors flashed by—a mix of the deep greens of pine trees and lighter-colored aspens gave way to fields with knee-high grasses and open pastures with herds of cattle grazing. He'd loved spending time in the woods as a kid, always a little removed from his younger siblings. He'd been quiet and studious, making mischief in his own way but nowhere near the hell-raising Josh, Logan and Beth had been a part of in their youth.

Jake was almost eight years older than the twins. By the time they came along, he already had dreams of leaving the life he knew behind. Their father had been a mean drunk and their mother had stayed devoted to him even when things were the worst. On the surface, it would have appeared that Jake had nothing in common with his blue-collar father. Nothing except that Jake was the spitting image of Billy Travers. Billy had always told Jake that he was going to grow up to be just like him. He knew his dad must have meant it as a compliment, but it had scared the hell out of Jake. Billy took credit for Jake's talent in math and science, claiming that his future had been just as bright until Janet had gotten pregnant with Jake at seventeen.

Jake didn't believe it was true. His father had drunk away any promise of his future and that had nothing to do with Billy's family. But Jake had been terrified into believing it could go the other way, that he could grow up into the same kind of spiteful, bitter man his father was. So he'd left Crimson and never looked back, even when things had gotten worse in his family. Even when the twins reached high school and he'd heard about their wild streak. Even when it had become clear that his little sister was out of control.

By the time Jake had been ready to intervene, it was too late. Beth had been killed in a car accident caused by a drunk driver. Logan didn't want anything to do with him, and Josh had been consumed with his life on the rodeo circuit. Jake had been finishing his residency at the time, sleep deprived and stressed. So he hadn't even tried to pull his family back together.

He'd failed his brothers. Now when he'd finally returned, he couldn't stand to take their support, no matter how much he needed it. The sound of Brooke singing sweetly from the backseat penetrated his mind, pulling him back into the present.

All of this was for her, he reminded himself. It didn't matter how hard it was for him. Brooke was his only priority.

He rolled his head along the seat rest until he faced Millie. "I'll go to dinner tonight," he told her. "For Brooke's sake."

Chapter Six

Jake was afraid he might grind his teeth to dust before the night was over. He forced the smile to remain on his face as he sat at the table between Brooke and his sister-in-law Sara.

He knew Millie had thought a big family dinner would be a good distraction, but thanks to the way his brothers were fawning all over him, he couldn't focus on anything except his injuries.

It was a perfect summer evening. The temperature this high in the mountains was warm but comfortable. A refreshing breeze blew up from the river that edged the far side of the property. They were eating outside on the big back patio of the main house on Crimson Ranch. The view of the mountains was so incredible, Jake could see why families would choose this place for their vacations.

According to Josh, the most recent group of guests had left earlier in the afternoon and the next batch would arrive two days from now. It was only family on the ranch tonight.

Brooke put down the last bite of her hamburger, her eyes scanning the table and the ground around her chair. "I left Bunny inside."

Jake thought it was a good sign that his daughter had forgotten her stuffed animal, even for a few minutes.

"I'll get him for you." Jake pushed away from the table.

"No, let me," Josh offered quickly.

"I can do it," Logan said.

Josh scrambled to his feet at the same time as Logan.

Jake froze, watching his brothers.

Millie let out a disbelieving laugh. "How many tall, strapping men does it take to retrieve a stuffed rabbit?"

There was a moment of awkward silence at the table.

"I'm finished eating," Claire, Josh's daughter, finally said. Claire was almost fourteen and it had been adoration at first sight for Brooke. "Brooke, why don't we get Bunny and go up to my room? I'll paint your nails."

"Can I go, Daddy?" Brooke turned to Jake.

"Sure thing." He glanced at Claire. "Thank you."

"It's cool." Claire smiled. "I like having a little cousin."

A lot more than he liked having two younger brothers at the moment.

Olivia stood as the girls went into the house. "Logan made his famous brownies tonight."

"I've got ice cream that will go great with it," Sara said as she jumped up from her seat. "I'll go in with you."

He watched Olivia give a meaningful look to Millie. "Would you make coffee to go with dessert?"

He glanced at Josh and Logan, both of whom were stacking plates and handing them to their wives. They must have planned time alone with him. Just what he needed, some sort of family intervention.

Millie got out of her chair slowly. "I'm pretty sure you don't need me to make the coffee," he heard her mumble under her breath.

He could tell she was torn between her reluctance to be shuffled off with the wives and not wanting to appear rude to their hosts.

As she followed Sara and Olivia into the house, Jake took a drink of his beer.

"Is alcohol allowed with your meds?" Josh looked concerned.

"It's one beer." Jake took a deliberately long pull from it.

"How about a glass of water?" Logan asked.

"You two..." Millie sounded frustrated as she stalked back to the table, still carrying empty dishes. "What's the problem? He's having a drink."

Josh's mouth thinned. "Jake doesn't drink."

"Never," Logan added.

"You mean in high school?" she asked. "So what? Not everyone did. He's an adult now. Legal age." She set the plates on the table and plopped down into her chair, clearly not willing to be brushed off so easily. "Give the mother-hen routine a rest, guys."

She looked fierce, her eyes gleaming as she stared down his brothers, both of whom were more than twice her size. His little Fairy Poppins had a backbone of steel, he realized. It felt good to have someone in his corner, sticking up for him—even if she didn't understand why Josh and Logan were so disturbed by him having a beer.

"Our father was an alcoholic," he said quietly, reaching out to lay his hand on the nape of her neck. It felt good to touch her, grounding in a way he needed right now. "He always said I was going to grow up to be just like him."

Millie's big eyes clashed with his. "But you're not..."

He shook his head. "I guess it was because I looked so much like him. Or because I was quiet in the same way he was. Who knows? But I took it that he meant he expected me to become a drunk like him. For that reason, I vowed never to touch alcohol."

Logan sat forward across the table. "He made us do some kind of weird blood-brothers handshake to solidify it."

Jake almost smiled at the bittersweet memory. "Damn, you and Beth were probably only seven years old at the time."

"All I remember is that Jake was thrilled at the prospect of all of us being cut so he could patch us up after." Josh looked at Millie. "He always wanted to be a doctor. Carried a first-aid kit around with him everywhere."

"That's because you guys and your idiot friends were always getting hurt."

"Blood brothers?" Millie's voice sounded a little faint.

Jake held out his palm to display the tiny crescent scar at its base. Logan and Josh did the same.

"Beth wouldn't do it," Logan said then chuckled. "Oh, wait, I forgot. Millie has the same issue with blood that Beth did. I found her in Olivia's kitchen a few months ago almost passed out from the sight of a little blood."

Jake noticed that the color had washed out of her cheeks. "Are you okay?"

She swallowed then nodded. "I can handle talking about blood. Just like you can handle a couple of beers. Right?"

"I realized several years back that I'm not like our father." *In that respect,* Jake added silently.

"Then get off his back," she said to Josh and Logan,

pointing a finger at each of them. "You can't expect him to abide by every vow he took when you were kids."

"We're worried." Josh crossed his arms over his chest.

"We want to help," Logan added. "The accident scared the hell out of us, Jake. This may not be a tight-knit family, but you're still our brother. Tell us what you need."

A miracle, he wanted to answer. Because the truth was he didn't know what the hell he needed. To rewind the past and keep Stacy from dying. To know he was going to be able to do surgery again once his hand and leg healed. To understand the first thing about being a father. "Just give me some time."

"You can stay, you know." Josh fiddled with his beer bottle as he spoke. "In Crimson. It's a good town to raise a kid. To make a home."

Home. The word echoed in the silence for several seconds. Jake realized that was what both of his brothers had done. They'd made a home in this town, despite all of the history and tangled memories that still surrounded Crimson from their childhood.

"I'm here for now," Jake answered. "That's all I can tell you. Don't push me for something more."

He rubbed his fingers against his forehead, where a dull pounding beat a steady rhythm against his skull.

Millie took a deep breath next to him. "Actually, the talk about blood did make my stomach kind of queasy." She turned to him. "Would you mind if we went back to the house now?"

Her eyes didn't give away anything, but he doubted that she wanted to leave because her stomach hurt. She knew he was at the end of his ability to keep up any semblance of being social. Hell, she understood him better than anyone else in the world at this moment. It made him feel weak that he couldn't even handle an entire evening with his family. But he couldn't deny the truth of it.

"I'll get Brooke," he said and pushed back from the table.

At close to eleven that night, Millie threw off her covers and climbed out of bed, pausing in the doorway of her bedroom. She'd been in and out of bed at least a half dozen times since she'd tucked Brooke in when they returned home from dinner at the ranch.

Jake hadn't said much on the drive back to the house, and she wondered whether she'd overstepped the bounds by inserting herself into his conversation with Josh and Logan. She knew the brothers meant well, but it had also been obvious that being the center of all that smothering attention wasn't helping Jake in the least.

Brooke had wanted Jake to read her a story after she'd said good-night to Millie. At first he'd protested, saying Millie could do the job of putting Brooke to bed better than he. But once he'd been in the room, propped against the headboard with his daughter snuggled to his side, she'd seen the tension ease out of his shoulders. Even though he couldn't see it, he needed his young daughter as much as she needed him.

It had felt foolish to wait around for Jake to be finished. What was she going to say to him anyway, especially after telling his brothers to leave him alone?

She'd retreated to her room, but had left the light on at first and the door open a crack—in case he'd wanted to seek her out. He hadn't, of course. Such a guy.

She could still hear the muffled sounds of the television and hated how much she craved his company, even after being there for only a short time. An idea rooted in her brain about Jake's issues with Crimson and his reluctance to make any sort of plan for the future. It was a flimsy excuse, perhaps, but as Millie padded toward the family room she told herself that this was a conversation they should have when Brooke wasn't within earshot.

One soft table lamp and the glow from the television were the only things that lit the family room. A loud crash sounded from the TV, making her jump. An old Bruce Willis action movie was playing. Jake was sitting on the couch, his booted foot propped up on the coffee table.

She paused in the kitchen, the tile floor cool under her feet. The window above the sink was open and a summer breeze blew in, making goose bumps rise on her arms. Doubts flooded her mind and almost had her turning around to retreat back to her bedroom. Nothing about being so close to Jake late at night in this darkened house was a good idea.

Before she could move, the sound clicked off from the TV.

"You can come all the way over," he said quietly. "I won't bite."

Silly that her heart was beating so frantically. She came around the corner of the couch, suddenly wishing her gauzy summer pajamas were made of heavier fabric. "How did you know I was standing there?"

"I've been waiting for you." Jake hit a button on the remote and his face was thrown into shadow.

Millie perched on the corner of the sofa nearest the table lamp, only a few feet from Jake but close to the only light source in the room. She wasn't ready to be in the dark with him.

Jake didn't look at her but picked up a glass from the sofa's armrest, swirling the clear liquid and ice before taking a long drink. "It's club soda, if you were wondering," he said after a moment.

"I wasn't."

Now he did turn to her, his gaze disbelieving. "Really? After everything you heard tonight, you aren't the least bit concerned that I'm going to turn into a drunken, pill-popping wreck thanks to the accident? That's how it really started with my dad. He'd been drinking forever, but he was off work for a while after he fell from a ladder on a job site and hurt his back. He did construction and odd jobs. But from that time, the work was more sporadic and the drinking more regular. I could be a real chip off the old block. That's what Jake and Logan think, the basis for all of their concern."

She shook her head. "I think you're using your father's issues as a convenient excuse to avoid facing what's happened to you. I think you like throwing your brothers off the scent of the real problem."

One of his brows rose. "Which is?"

"How scared you are of failing."

She saw his left hand ball into a fist. "Look at me, Millie. Don't you think I've already failed?"

"At what?"

After a moment he whispered, "I couldn't save Stacy."

Millie inched closer, propelled by frustration and temper. "You're not invincible, Jake. What happened to her was a tragic accident. But she chose to come to the island, even knowing how unstable things were. That decision was on her." When he started to speak, she held up a hand. "And no, I don't think you know much about failure. Trust me, I'm a bit of an expert. I bet you haven't failed at a single thing in your entire life. Because instead you run away when things get too hard. You take the easy way out."

"Easy way?" His eyes narrowed. "I put myself through college and medical school on my own. I am…I was a damn good surgeon. I go to places most people couldn't imagine. You think that's easy?"

She shrugged. "I didn't say you aren't willing to work hard. But I know you're smart." She lifted her hand to make air quotes. "Valedictorian of your class." She was baiting him now, probably unfairly, but she had a feeling this might be the only way to break through his defenses. "I think you used your intelligence to break out of this town, and there's nothing wrong with that. But you sacrificed your relationships with your brothers in the process. As a girl who grew up without any siblings, I can tell you how much I wanted someone to truly understand what I had to go through as a kid."

"I get that." He dropped his head to the back of the couch, exposing the tanned skin of his neck and throat. Stubble shadowed his jaw, making him look both tired and a little more rugged than she was used to.

"You might be a brilliant surgeon," she continued, fighting to keep her voice steady, "but you chose a career path that almost guarantees you won't form long-term relationships with people. You said yourself that you go wherever you're needed, your bags are always packed. So it might be challenging and stressful, but you can manage it. Having a daughter is different. A potentially career-ending injury is different."

"You think I don't know that?"

"I think you aren't willing to face it. Because for the first time in your life the things that are on the line really matter. If you fail at this, the stakes are off-the-charts high. That's scary, I know. But not dealing with the fear isn't going to make it go away, Jake."

He moved his foot off the coffee table and leaned

forward, elbows on his knees, his hands pressing either side of his head. "So now you're a kid whisperer *and* an armchair psychiatrist?"

"I'm actually sitting on the sofa."

He lowered one hand, turning to her, a ghost of a smile playing on his lips. "A comedian as well. Lucky me."

"Am I right?"

He drew in a breath then blew it out. "Even if you are, what am I going to do about it?"

"*We're* going to make a plan."

His smile widened. "I thought you weren't the planning type, Millie."

"The plan is for you." She fluttered her fingers in the air. "I'm a free spirit. That's how my mother raised me."

"Bull."

"Excuse me?" She shook her head. "Ask anyone who knows me. I don't like to be tied down..." She frowned as his mouth quirked. "But not because I'm running away. I like change and movement, being flexible."

He rolled his eyes.

"But this isn't about me." She pointed a finger at him. "It's about you. And Brooke. You have to commit to her, Jake."

"I brought her to Colorado."

"That's an extended trip, not a commitment."

Jake stared at her for several long moments. Millie had hit the nail on the head with that comment. He'd brought his daughter to Crimson because he'd made a promise to a dying woman, not because he suddenly had fantastic parental instincts. In the back of Jake's mind, he still believed Brooke would be better off with her grandparents. He could visit when his schedule allowed, maybe plan a few trips around her school schedule once she got old enough.

He didn't truly think he had more to give than that. "What do you expect me to do?"

"How long until your injuries heal?"

"They want me to do physical therapy for another four weeks. By then, the nerves should have healed enough to know whether there's permanent damage." He paused then added, "Enough impairment to end a career anyway."

"Your decision about being a full-time father to Brooke shouldn't be based on whether or not you can perform surgery. She isn't a second-string priority."

"You think I don't know that, Millie?"

Her voice softened. "You need to give being a parent a real shot. Commit to trying, to making it work. If not and you let someone else raise her, as wonderful as Brooke's grandparents might be, you'll always wonder if you could have done more."

"I have been giving this a real shot." He gestured to the row of toys Millie had organized earlier along the far wall of the family room. "I have twenty-gazillion pounds of pink plastic cluttering a rental house in a town I never expected to see again. Doesn't that count as a real try?"

"Halloween."

"What about Halloween?"

"I want you to promise you'll stay with Brooke until then. It gives you over two full months together. You need to stay, no matter what you hear about your injuries. Even if her grandparents arrive and try to convince you that she'd be better off with them."

He gave a harsh laugh. "It's like you know Stacy's parents already."

"I know that all of you have been through something tragic." She shifted closer and placed her fingers on his wrist. "I also know that the relationship you have with your daughter will affect her for the rest of her life."

He lost himself for a moment in her bright eyes. Once again, this tiny pixie of a woman made him want to try to be the kind of man he wasn't sure existed inside him. "No pressure."

"I know you're scared to fail her."

He stared at her fingers on his arm, her nails brightly colored against his skin. Slowly, he lifted her fingers, lining up his hand with hers, palm to palm. Her fingers barely came past his knuckles—that was how tiny her hand was in his. "Did your father fail you, Millie?" he asked.

He felt her hand stiffen against his, and he laced their fingers together before she could pull away. "My father is an example of the point I'm trying to make. You can't fail if you don't try." Her eyes clouded with sadness. "It will be so much worse for Brooke if she grows up believing she wasn't worth the effort. That I know for sure."

An ache sliced through him for the little girl Millie used to be, the one who never believed she was worthy of her father's attention. He might be afraid, but Jake would never give that burden to his daughter. He lifted his other hand and traced the line of her jaw with two fingers. His hand might go numb at regular intervals and he didn't know if he'd ever be able to perform another surgery, but at this moment the feel of Millie's soft skin under the tips of his fingers seemed like all he needed in the world.

Her eyes fell closed and it felt like an invitation. He leaned closer and brushed his mouth across hers, savoring her softness as her breath mingled with his. "So sweet," he murmured, moving his hand to the back of her neck to bring her nearer to him.

She wrapped her arms around his shoulders and gave

the tiniest moan in the back of her throat. The sound brought parts of his body to full attention. Never had Jake been so affected by a woman. He was all for mutual pleasure, but the innate need thundering through his veins was something wholly new for him. It felt as though everything about Millie Spencer was made to entice him, from the way she smelled like springtime flowers to the softness of her skin.

She was an intoxicating mix of strength and vulnerability wrapped up in a package of feminine grace. "Your father was an idiot," he whispered against her mouth. "You're worth the effort, Millie. This is worth it all."

He'd meant the words as a compliment, but she suddenly jumped to her feet, tugging at the hem of her pajama top. "We can't do this," she said, a look of panic in her eyes. "You can't do this, Jake."

He stood and reached for her but she backed away. "It was a kiss, Millie. That's all. I don't think I was the only one who was enjoying it, either."

She shook her head, looking miserable. "I'm not that kind of woman."

"What kind of woman?" He felt his temper kick in. What the hell was she talking about?

"The kind that… You can't… We can't…" She squeezed her eyes shut. "I work for you, Jake. That's all."

"And you think I'm assuming this is a perk of paying you. That you have to watch my kid and then service me when she goes to bed. Is that what you think of me, Millie?"

"No. I didn't mean—"

"Forget it." He scrubbed his hand over his face. "The kiss never happened. It wasn't part of the bargain. I get it. No matter what happens with my recovery, I'm here until Halloween. I'm going all-in with Brooke although

I still highly doubt I'm her best bet." *That I'm anyone's best bet,* he thought to himself. "But I'm going to try. If I fail, then at least I gave it a shot. That's what you want, right?"

She nodded, pulling on her lower lip with her teeth. She didn't look at him, though. One damned kiss and she couldn't even make eye contact.

"You got your way. Congratulations." He stepped around her. "I hope you know what you're doing."

Chapter Seven

Millie had no idea what she was doing. She lay in bed the next morning replaying the events of the previous night over in her head. Jake had kissed her. She'd wanted him to; there was no doubt about it. The minute his mouth had touched hers, her whole body came to life. His claim that she'd "enjoyed" it was an understatement, to say the least. The kiss had tilted her world on its axis and she wasn't sure she could right it again.

But she had to try. She was going to deny her attraction to Jake Travers no matter what. Not only because she worked for him, but to prove she could deny it. Millie was determined not to be like her mother, who'd turned every interaction she had with men into something calculating. As much as her mom was always the fun, good-time girl, she also used her sexuality as a weapon to manipulate men. It had slowly chipped away at her self-worth in the process.

Millie would not be that person. She was going to

stand on her own two feet, even when the ground beneath her was mucky and unstable.

With that thought spurring her on, she got dressed, then headed to the kitchen to get started on the French toast before Brooke woke up. To her surprise, Jake was already standing at the stove, his daughter setting plates and forks at the table.

"Good morning," she said as her feet touched the tile. "You two are up early."

"Daddy's making quesadillas," Brooke sang out. "He can cook, Millie. And not just delivery pizza."

"Quesadillas?" She glanced at Jake and willed the color to stop creeping up her cheeks.

"Breakfast quesadillas," he clarified. "Have a seat, ladies. They're almost ready."

She sat in the chair Brooke held out for her but wanted to escape back into her bedroom. As much as the quiet intimacy of last night had shaken her, watching Jake in all his domestic glory was just as unsettling. He wore another pair of loose athletic shorts and a faded University of Colorado T-shirt that stretched across the muscles of his back and shoulders. His hair was tousled from sleep and a shadow of stubble covered his jaw.

Why was it so damned appealing to watch a man in the kitchen? Or maybe she was just over her head with this particular man.

She took a quick sip of her juice as he came to the table, unable to make eye contact with him for fear he'd be able to read in her eyes the lie that she'd told him last night. Her brain might want to keep their relationship professional, but her body had ideas of its own.

He slid a few sections of quesadilla from the pan to her plate and she watched as he did the same for Brooke, unable to look away from the movement of his hands.

Maybe she should have started the day with a cold shower.

There was a bowl with sliced fruit in the middle of the table, so she distracted herself by spooning some out for each of them.

"Coffee?" Jake asked, his voice tinged with humor.

She glanced up at him then and he raised his brows, as if he could read every inappropriate thought in her mind. "Thanks," she muttered as he filled her cup.

"The breakfast-dillas are yum-mo," Brooke said as she took another big bite. She reached out to pat Millie's arm. "We can make Frenchy toast tomorrow, right?"

Jake folded himself into the chair next to Brooke. "Did you say *French toes*?" He leaned closer to his daughter. "I can't eat French toes. What if the feet weren't washed first?" He mock shuddered and Brooke dissolved into a fit of giggles.

"Daddy, you're so silly." She licked at the cheese dripping from her quesadilla. "But you make good breakfast."

"I'm glad you like it," he answered then smiled at Millie. "What do you think?"

She could read the challenge in his gaze. "An A for effort," she admitted then took a small bite of one wedge. It was a perfect combination of egg and cheese with the tortilla grilled to a crispy golden brown. "It's actually pretty good. Where did you learn to make these?"

"I did a stint in a little village in southern Mexico called Chiapas. I learned to get creative with eggs and tortillas."

"I thought you didn't cook."

He shrugged. "My skills are limited, but I'm trying."

Suddenly his gaze wasn't teasing or challenging. It was hopeful and open and almost knocked Millie to the floor. She realized that when Jake Travers really tried at something, there was probably very little he couldn't accomplish. Like making her heart open to him.

"Mommy said breakfast was the most important meal of the day." Brooke set Bunny on the empty chair and spread a napkin in front of him. She broke off a small piece of quesadilla and laid it on the napkin along with a strawberry.

Jake's jaw went slack as he stared at his daughter.

Millie filled the silence. "You learned a lot of really smart stuff from your mommy."

Brooke nodded and took a sip of juice.

"What do you have planned for today after your therapy appointment?" Millie asked Jake.

He looked at her as if it was a trick question.

"I made a call to the preschool Natalie Holt recommended. Brooke is going to visit the classroom, and the director has time today after lunch to talk about enrollment. I was hoping you could be there, too. It's your decision, after all."

"My decision," he repeated.

"I don't want to go to school. My friends aren't there." Brooke crumpled the napkin and grabbed on to her stuffed rabbit, pulling him close to her chest. "I want to stay with Daddy."

Her big eyes filled with tears. Millie could feel Jake's resistance crumbling.

"How about we just give it a try?" she coaxed. "You and your daddy can decide if it's right for you once you take a look and meet the teacher." Millie smiled. "After that we can visit Katie at Life Is Sweet for a homemade cookie."

The girl perked up at that. "Chocolate chip?"

"Of course," Millie promised.

"Okay. I'll try it." She scrunched up her nose. "But I probably won't want to stay." She hopped off her seat. "I'm finished. Can I have screen time now?"

"Sure," Jake answered immediately.

She skipped away toward the front of the house, where the office was located.

"Great attitude," Millie said when she was gone. "Wonder where she gets it?"

"How do you avoid the big meltdowns with her?" Jake shook his head. "I swear she was crying every other minute before you got here. I live in constant fear of those tears."

"Believe it or not, kids want a schedule and rules. It helps ground them." She waved her hand at the table. "Looks like having a plan has made a difference to you already."

"Two months. I'm giving it my all for two months. We'll see what happens after that."

"You sound like Brooke and her thoughts on preschool. But I have great faith in both of you."

Jake gave a small laugh. "Which brings up a good point. I don't know anything about choosing a preschool, Millie. You're the one with the teaching degree—"

"Not yet," she corrected. "Remember I'm on a break from school. Who knows if I'll even go back." She stood quickly, grabbing the plates from the table. What had possessed her to share that little tidbit with him?

Keeping her back to Jake, she rinsed the dishes in the sink.

"Afraid of failure?" came a voice in her ear a few moments later. She whirled around, still holding the nozzle of the kitchen sprayer.

"Whoa!" Jake jumped out of the line of fire with a

laugh just as she let go of the sprayer. "Be careful where you point that thing."

"I'm not afraid of failure." Millie tried to keep her words steady, but couldn't help the slight catch in her voice. "And I'm *not* running away."

"I didn't say you were."

She turned back to the sink and flipped off the water.

"Hey." Jake placed a hand on her shoulder. She continued to focus her gaze on the stainless steel in front of her. "I was joking, Millie. I know this is about me." He paused then added, "I'm sorry for last night. I don't want to take advantage of you or make you uncomfortable."

She waved off his concern. "It's okay. It was probably my fault. I know I—"

Now he did spin her around. "You did nothing wrong," he said, bending so he could look into her eyes. His were so blue and honest she couldn't help but nod.

"You either. It was a moment. It happened. We got it out of our systems."

He brought his face within inches of hers. "Are you sure about that?"

She forced herself to nod and he stepped back, straightening. "Good to know." He turned and collected the rest of the dishes. When the kitchen was cleaned, Jake walked to his bedroom to change clothes for his appointment.

Millie drove him to the hospital, but this time, Brooke was okay letting him out at the doors by the main entrance.

He said goodbye and climbed out of the Explorer. Before shutting the door, he turned back to Millie. "For the record, I didn't get anything out of my system last night," he said. "Just so you know."

Millie sucked in a breath, but he disappeared before she could answer.

* * *

Jake cradled his wrist in his good arm as he left the physical-therapy office two hours later. The exercises left him feeling both reinvigorated and exhausted, hopeful that he was making progress and frustrated that it wasn't faster or easier.

He took the elevator to the ground floor of the hospital and started toward the front entrance, where Millie and Brooke would pick him up. His name was called and he turned to the sound. A woman and a man, both in white lab coats, walked toward him.

"Lana?"

The tall brunette smiled at him. "I heard you were in town."

He shook his head. "What are you doing in Crimson?"

"Finishing up my fellowship," Lana Mayfield answered. "And getting lucky enough to cross paths with my favorite med-school study partner again." She turned to the man standing next to her. "Jake, I want to introduce you to Vincent Gile, the medical director at Rocky Mountain West."

The older man held out a hand. "It's a pleasure to meet you. You're a bit of a legend around here."

Jake shook Vincent's hand. "I don't understand..."

"The people of Crimson are extremely proud of their world-traveling Dr. Travers. You'd be surprised how many patients ask if I've met you." The man chuckled. "Like the medical community is one big social-media outlet. But I'm happy to finally put a face with your name and list of accomplishments."

"My list of..."

"Don't be modest, Jake." Lana shook her finger at him. "First in our class graduating from med school then on to your charity work all around the globe. You've got quite a reputation."

"We were all sorry to hear about your injuries," Vincent added. "I want you to know we'll take good care of you here at West. If there's anything you need, just let me know." He took a step closer. "I also hope you'll let me take you to lunch while you're in town. Crimson is a great place to live, as I'm sure you know. Now that you're back, I'd like to talk to you about a possible future here."

Jake felt his mouth drop open. "That's kind of you. But as I'm sure you're aware, I don't know the long-term effects of the accident yet. There's a chance..."

Vincent waved away Jake's concerns. "If you're interested, we'll find a place for you. A local doctor on staff, especially one as well respected in the community as you, is not something I'd pass on, I can tell you that."

The man's cell phone beeped. "I have a meeting. How about lunch next week?"

"Sure," Jake answered, stunned at Vincent Gile's interest in him.

"I look forward to it." The cell phone beeped again. "Gotta run." With a quick nod to Lana, Vincent turned and headed back toward the elevator. Jake and Lana watched him go.

When the metal doors closed, Jake let out a long breath. "Is he always like that?"

"Intense and direct?" Lana laughed. "Absolutely." Her expression turned serious. "He manages a great hospital for someplace so remote."

"Remote? I wouldn't call Crimson remote."

She smiled. "I did both medical school and my residency in Chicago. Remember? This place moves like molasses compared to what I'm used to."

"You don't like it here?"

"It's fine for now," she said with a shrug of her delicate

shoulders. She reached forward and gave him a quick hug. "I like it better now that you're in town."

"Thanks." Jake didn't know how else to respond. He'd met Lana his second year of med school. He'd managed to graduate from college in three and a half years and applied directly to medical school from there. He'd been young and hungry to prove that he could handle the rigors of med school, but it had been a challenge. He'd received scholarships but still had to work part-time at a neighborhood diner to pay for books and expenses. That didn't leave much time for any type of a social life. Lana had been just as ambitious, only her motivation was to prove to her neurosurgeon father that she'd inherited his talent.

They'd become study partners and dated casually, mostly because neither had the time or energy to make a real relationship work. They'd ended up at the same hospital for residency, but lost touch when their careers had taken them on separate paths.

When he'd first met her, Lana had been the exact opposite of everything Jake had grown up with in Crimson. She was sophisticated, confident and coolly beautiful. The years hadn't changed that. Unlike most of the doctors he'd met in Crimson, who adopted a mountain-casual look even while on the clock, Lana wore an expensive and exquisitely tailored suit under her lab coat. Her hair was glossy, pulled back into a smooth ponytail at the nape of her neck.

For a moment an image of Millie's sprite-like tumble of hair came to his mind. Strange that he'd think of Millie while talking to Lana.

"I missed you after you moved on," she said now, bringing him back to reality.

"Yeah, sorry." He remembered that she'd texted him

after graduation. "I was traveling so much, it was hard to keep up with friends."

She dipped her chin and smiled at him. "I get off at six. Let's have dinner and catch up. I want to hear all about your adventures." She placed a hand on his arm. "My fellowship is over at the end of September. I was thinking I might like to try something new. Maybe with Miles of Medicine. It would be fun to coordinate our schedules." She gave his arm a squeeze. "Like the old days."

The old days when all he had to worry about was ingesting enough caffeine to keep up with his round-the-clock shifts. A day with Brooke made overnights during his residency look like a cakewalk.

"I've got a lot going on right now and doubt I'll be decent company by the end of the day," he said, not mentioning that most of his fatigue came from the responsibility of parenthood. "Another time."

Her smile dropped a bit but she nodded. "Definitely. It's good to see you, Jake." She reached up on her tiptoes and gave him a kiss on his cheek. "You make this town suddenly seem much more interesting."

He took a step back. The gleam in her eye made him a little nervous. "See you around, Lana." He walked quickly out of the hospital, dropping his sunglasses over his eyes as he did.

He spotted the Explorer parked near the edge of the patient-drop-off area. As he got closer, he could hear music coming from the open windows. It wasn't a song he recognized, although the melody sounded vaguely familiar. Brooke's high-pitched, little-girl voice was belting out song lyrics. He stopped in his tracks as Millie joined her.

Millie's voice was just like her—bright and bubbly—

and totally mesmerizing as she harmonized with the tune Brooke was singing.

He opened the car door and started to speak, but Millie held up one finger. "This is the big finale," she whispered on a quick breath before singing again.

A glance to the back of the car showed Brooke with her eyes closed, a rapturous look on her face as she continued to sing, blissfully unaware of his return.

A man in scrubs wheeled an elderly woman past the car and they both turned to look at Millie, who waved cheerfully.

"Do you want to roll up the windows for this?" Jake asked.

She ignored him, her voice rising to join Brooke's at the end of the song.

Despite himself, Jake felt chills roll down his back. Her voice was like a caress as she sang about playing all day in the sun.

After a few moments, the song ended and Millie flipped off the volume on the radio control.

"That was awesome," she said, turning to give Brooke a high five. "You are the best Ariel I've ever heard."

"You sound just like a princess," Brooke answered, and Jake could see Millie's stock rise several notches in his daughter's estimation.

"*The Little Mermaid* was my favorite movie when I was a kid," she told Jake, easing into the parking lot. "I combed my hair with a fork for months after seeing it the first time." She was practically bouncing in her seat. "How was your appointment? Did it run late?"

He blinked several times to keep up with the various conversation threads. "I saw someone I knew from my residency. And why would you comb your hair with a fork?"

"Daddy doesn't watch princess movies," Brooke said from the backseat.

"Everyone watches princess movies. We'll rent one tonight." Millie wiggled her eyebrows at Jake. "You'll love it."

"I can't wait." The funny part was Jake realized he meant it.

Millie and Brooke took turns telling him about their morning until they pulled in front of a small brick house on one of the side streets leading from downtown.

"This looks lovely," Millie murmured.

She was right. The brick on the house's exterior was painted a pale yellow with dark blue trim and shutters. Planter boxes hung under the windows, and the flowers each held were cheerful, as if they were giving a warm welcome to each person who walked up the path that led to the front door.

"I don't want to do this," Brooke said quietly from the backseat.

Me neither, Jake agreed silently as he watched a group of mothers trickle up the sidewalk, kids in tow.

"It's just a visit," Millie reminded Brooke. "You're brave like a princess, Brookie-Cookie." She gave Jake a meaningful look, as if he was supposed to add something more to the conversation.

He got out of the SUV and opened the back door. "I'll hold your hand the whole time," he offered without thinking, then felt like an idiot. Why would that matter?

To his surprise, Brooke nodded. "Okay, Daddy. As long as you don't leave me."

He smiled. "I'll be right here."

Taking her hand in his, Jake led Brooke toward the front door of the house, Millie at his side. "Tell me again why you can't just teach her what she needs to know," he whispered.

"This is about socialization and her development." She glanced around him to Brooke. "It's important for her to have time away from you."

"She does," he argued. "When I'm at the hospital."

Millie shook her head and gave him a gentle elbow to the ribs. "It's just a visit."

A woman who looked to be around fifty years old greeted them. Silver hair just grazed her shoulders. She wore an apron with the words Crimson Community Preschool in block lettering across the front. If Jake had to imagine what an ideal preschool teacher would look like, this woman was it. Her face was kind, her smile gentle as she held out her hand. "I'm Ms. Laura," she said, speaking directly to his daughter. "Are you Brooke?"

Brooke nodded and took a small step forward. "This is Bunny. He's scared, so he has to stay with me."

Ms. Laura patted the stuffed animal on the head. "It's nice to meet you, Bunny," she answered without missing a beat. She turned her gaze to Jake and Millie.

"Thanks so much for letting us come by today," Millie said quickly. "We spoke on the phone. I'm Millie Spencer, the nanny, and this is Brooke's father, Jake Travers."

"Laura Wilkes," the woman responded. "Welcome to all of you." She pointed to a doorway off the entry of the house. "Why don't you take a look around? School starts next week, so we do small group orientations to talk to the children about how their day will go. We have two new additions to the older class, so Brooke won't be the only one joining us."

"We're just visiting." Brooke spoke to Bunny, not making eye contact with the teacher.

"That's fine." Laura Wilkes bent down to Brooke's

level. “If you and your daddy like it here, Brooke, I hope you’ll come back. I think you’d enjoy our time together.”

Jake felt his daughter’s grip tighten on his hand even as she inched forward. “Let’s go, Daddy.”

He took several steps toward the main room of the preschool before he realized Millie wasn’t following him. “Are you coming?” he asked, glancing over his shoulder at her.

She gave him a reassuring smile. “In a minute. You two go ahead.” She turned back to Laura, and Jake allowed himself to be led into the room, certain that Millie was purposely hanging back so he and Brooke would do this on their own.

His throat went dry as he took in the colorful tables with blocks and building equipment. An art station was situated near the center of the room, complete with easels and paints. In the corner was a play kitchen, shelves of neatly stacked food near one side.

The four mothers in the room all turned as he and Brooke walked in. A couple of the kids looked over and he felt Brooke stiffen next to him. He was pretty sure he and his daughter shared the same instinct at this moment, which was to get the hell out of there. Instead, he plastered a smile on his face.

“Hi,” he said, lifting his splinted arm in a wave. “I’m Jake and this is my daughter, Brooke. We’re new to Crimson and visiting the preschool today.”

The women stared at him for a few moments, then descended like a litter of puppies on a new toy. Introductions were made as they drew him forward. Jake found that when Brooke’s hand began to slip from his, he was the one holding on tight.

“It’s okay, Daddy.” She handed him Bunny. “I’m going

to play in the kitchen." He watched her follow another girl to the far side of the room.

Just like that, he was left alone. He gave another half-hearted smile. "I'm sort of new to being a dad," he admitted. "Brooke's been living with her mother up until a few weeks ago." He didn't bother to mention all that went into that statement, and the women didn't seem to care.

They extolled the virtues of the preschool and Ms. Laura to the point Jake felt as if he'd entered some tiny kid-sized cult. As he watched Brooke interact with the other kids in the room, smiling and laughing, he realized it might be worth it.

One of the moms shared that she was also a single parent and invited him to coffee to discuss tips for making it work. Jake backed away so fast he almost tripped over a beanbag chair behind him. Thankfully, Laura Wilkes walked into the room at that moment.

Millie was nowhere in sight. He wondered where his nanny had disappeared to and why she'd left him alone with this horde of overfriendly mothers.

"Friends," Laura said to the children scattered around the room, "let's gather on the carpet." The kids scampered forward as if this Ms. Laura was the Pied Piper. Talk about commanding a room. The preschool director, for all her sweetness, was definitely in charge.

He expected Brooke to find him, but she took a seat on the floor next to the girl she'd been playing with in the kitchen.

"It's funny," one of the mothers said quietly. "You spend so long wanting them to become more independent. Then it's hard when they do."

He nodded, unsure how else to answer. He hadn't spent *so long* wanting anything from Brooke, but somehow he understood exactly what the woman meant.

Laura explained the daily schedule for the school, the different types of learning environments, how the classroom changed and special events for the year, including a class musical to coincide with the Halloween party. He smiled at the look of utter rapture on his daughter's face as she listened intently to information about snack time, recess and different projects Ms. Laura had planned.

When the children and parents were released a half hour later, he wasn't surprised that Brooke came running up to him, quickly saying, "I'm going to do school here, Daddy."

"You like it that much?" A pang of disappointment shafted through him. He knew it was good that she felt comfortable at the school and he couldn't blame her. But even as he constantly felt unsure of himself as a father, Brooke's dependence on him was the only solid thing in his life right now.

"I love it," she assured him. "Bunny does, too." She took the stuffed animal from him and gave its scruffy head a big kiss.

Millie ducked into the classroom as Laura was walking the rest of the families out. "Pretty cool, right?" She bent and Brooke came forward to give her a big hug. "I'm proud of you, Cookie. You did great here today."

He wished he'd thought to say that. He wished he could show affection so naturally, but that had never been a part of Jake's makeup.

"Where were you?" He waved his hand around the room, unable to stop his irritation from spilling out. "This is your area of expertise and you left me to fend off the moms by myself."

Millie chuckled in response. "Oh, no. Not the moms," she said in mock horror. "I was filling out paperwork."

Oh. So she hadn't quite deserted him.

Laura Wilkes walked back into the room. "What did you think, Brooke?"

"Good," she answered. "Do I get my own cubby?"

Laura nodded. "And a shelf for your art projects. You can take Bunny on a tour of the rest of the room and across the hall where we have snack time while I talk to your daddy and Millie."

"You have a very sweet daughter," Laura said after Brooke left the room.

"I can't take credit for that," Jake answered.

Laura's smile was gentle. "Millie explained the situation to me. We'll take good care of her while she's at the preschool. Do you have any questions for me?"

"I wouldn't know where to start." Jake looked at Millie. "Do I have any questions?"

She shook her head. "Laura has been here over fifteen years. She has a wonderful philosophy for the children and most of what they learn is through hands-on play."

Jake looked at her blankly.

"That's good," she assured him.

"We use parent volunteers in the classroom," Laura added. "You're welcome to sign up out in the entry. I'll need a lot of help for the fall musical. My teaching partner also moved suddenly due to a family emergency. I'm interviewing this week and would love to have someone in place before school starts. If that doesn't happen, I'll be relying on volunteers even more until I can fill the position."

Jake nudged Millie, who only said, "Thanks for letting us come in today, Laura. I think this will be just what Brooke needs. We'll plan on seeing you the Tuesday after Labor Day for the first day of school."

She took a step toward the door, but stopped when Jake placed a hand on her arm. "You should hire Millie," he told Laura and heard Millie hiss out a breath. "She's a teacher."

"Not certified," Millie said quickly, frowning at Jake. "I haven't finished my degree yet."

Laura's face brightened. "We don't need someone certified for the teaching-assistant position. If you're interested, I'd love to talk to you about it."

Millie hesitated. "I'm not sure that I'd have the time with what Jake and Brooke need."

"We'll make it work." Jake shrugged at the glare Millie shot him.

"Okay…well…"

"Think about it," Laura told Millie. "Give me a call if you want to know more about the job. I have two candidates right now, but I'm not sure either of them is a good fit."

Millie nodded, but her mouth was grim. Jake didn't understand. He thought she'd be thrilled to have an opportunity to teach again. Hadn't Olivia told him how much her sister enjoyed working with kids?

They said goodbye and walked to the car.

"Don't ever do that to me again," Millie said under her breath as Brooke climbed into her car seat.

"Do what?" Jake was genuinely confused. "Try to help you?"

"I'm not the one who needs help." She crossed her arms over her chest. "My life is fine. I manage fine. I'll decide what kind of work I do and don't want. If you're looking to get rid of me, just say it, Jake."

He held up his hands. "I'm not trying to get rid of you, Millie. What would make you think—"

She shook her head. "Forget it." She closed her eyes, took a breath and opened them again, a sunny smile spreading across her face. "This was a huge success. The preschool is perfect for Brooke. The moms are going to love you. Everything's just great." She leaned into the car. "Who wants to celebrate at the bakery?"

"Me," Brooke shouted, raising both hands above her head.

"Let's go, then." After strapping Brooke's car seat, she shut the door and moved toward the driver's side.

Jake caught her arm. "What just happened there?"

"Nothing," she answered. But the smile was forced and didn't meet her eyes. Then her gaze softened. "Nothing, Jake. Please let it go."

After a moment, he nodded. "Okay. Let's get a cookie."

She exhaled, obviously relieved.

He would let it go for now, he thought as he got into the Explorer. But not for good. As sunny and bright as Millie appeared, there were shadows in her, a darkness she tried—but couldn't quite manage—to hide. Jake planned to find out what put it there.

Chapter Eight

Jake climbed the steps to his brother's house two days later, after Logan had picked him up from his latest visit to physical therapy.

"You're getting around better," Logan commented as he followed Jake up the stairs.

"Still worried you're going to have to break my fall when I lose my balance?"

"Not one bit."

Jake purposely fumbled then grinned as Logan scrambled to right him.

Jake straightened. "Liar."

Logan swore under his breath. "Next time, I'm going to let you go down."

Olivia opened the door as they came to the top. "He's all bark, no bite," she said as she held open the door, then followed him into the kitchen.

"Excuse me?" Logan put an arm around his wife's

waist and pulled her close. "Have you already forgotten last night?"

"Get a room," Jake muttered in a good-natured tone. He was happy for his brother. Logan had taken the death of their sister the hardest. Jake had tried to reach out years after Beth's death when Logan had seemed to be spiraling out of control. He'd wanted—albeit belatedly—to help his youngest brother come to terms with his grief, as if Jake was such an expert on that. But Logan hadn't wanted the interference of an older brother who'd left him and the rest of the family behind years ago. Jake had always wondered if Logan would make it to the other side of his pain in one piece and was grateful he seemed so content with his life since he'd returned to Crimson.

"Can I get you something to drink?" Olivia asked, playfully pushing Logan away. "I spoke with Millie earlier. She was taking Brooke to the children's museum over in Aspen this afternoon since you had plans with Logan."

He could hear the question in her voice. Jake had asked Logan to pick him up from the hospital, but actually wanted time to talk to Olivia.

"I want to know what's going on with your sister," he said, deciding it was best to cut straight to the point.

Olivia's delicate features took on a look of both confusion and concern. "Is something wrong with Millie? Do you have a problem with her? Is she not taking care of Brooke?" Her tone turned indignant. "Because I can tell she loves that little girl already. I've seen them together. I met them at the park yesterday and—"

"Sweetie, let him finish his thought." Logan smoothed the hair away from her face in an unconscious gesture.

Jake shook his head. "I don't have a problem with Millie."

The tension sagged out of Olivia's shoulders. "Sorry. It's weird. Millie and I are only now getting to know each other, but I feel very protective of her. She's my baby sister, you know?"

Jake's eyes flicked to Logan. "Yes, I know."

"Have a seat, Jake." Logan pulled out one of the high stools from the kitchen island.

"I'm worried about her," Jake said as he lowered himself into it. "There are things she's not telling me. Nothing to do with Brooke. She's fabulous with Brooke—different than I could ever be. Yet it works for all of us."

"She's got a gift with children."

"Which is my point. We were at the local preschool a few days ago. The director needs someone to help a few hours a day. It would be perfect for Millie."

"Early childhood education is her major."

"Right. But she wasn't interested. In fact, when I mentioned her background she all but bit off my head." He leaned forward. "Do you know the details of why she left school?"

Olivia shook her head. "Something happened at her student teaching assignment. I just figured Millie got bored of the day-to-day routine. She talks a lot about wanting her freedom and not making big commitments. It has to do with how she was raised, I think. Her mother was the ultimate free spirit." She gave a wry smile. "It's what drew my dad to her."

"Millie isn't her mother." Jake felt his temper flare.

"I know," Olivia answered quickly.

"For all her claims of being so footloose, she loves order and a schedule—at least on her own terms. She's got Brooke on a regular sleeping routine, limits her screen time, counts the fruit and vegetable servings she has each day. Hell, she has all of the toys in the house put away in their own special places each night. She can be fun and spontaneous, but she's also the most organized person I've ever met."

He shook his head. "It doesn't make sense that she would leave school and nothing explains why she wouldn't want the experience that the preschool can give her."

He looked up to find both Logan and Olivia staring at him.

"You just strung more words together than I've heard you speak in the past decade," Logan said, scratching his jaw.

"You care about her," Olivia added.

"She's responsible for my daughter," Jake said, unwilling to address his feelings. "Of course I care."

They both continued to watch him. "Don't read more into this than what it is. Brooke's grandparents arrive next week. Millie thinks she's going to turn me into the perfect father, but that's not going to happen." He looked to Logan for confirmation. "With our background, I'm not cut out to be a parent to anyone."

"Josh thought the same thing," Logan answered, "but he's doing fine with Claire."

"That's different." Jake straightened. "Josh was nothing like Dad."

"You're not like him, either."

Jake wanted to believe that but wasn't convinced.

"Josh and I are driving up the mountain today to do some maintenance near the trailhead above the ranch. Want to come with us?"

Jake held up his hand. "I'm not much help on the trail these days."

"We'll find some way for you to be useful."

He thought about going back to the empty house before Millie and Brooke returned then nodded. It had been years since he'd spent any time with his brothers. Part of him was worried they'd have nothing to talk about, but a larger piece didn't care. He'd spent so much time alone in his life. Even when he was working out in the field, Jake had always remained a little apart from the group. Being with his daughter and Millie had made him realize he liked feeling as if he belonged. Maybe he could learn how to translate that into a relationship with his brothers.

"Sure. I'd like that."

He was surprised at how happy his agreement seemed to make Logan.

"Are you and Millie bringing Brooke to the Labor Day Festival this weekend?" Olivia asked. "I'll be working a booth for the community center, and Sara and Josh will bring guests from the ranch. We can all meet up if that works?"

"The Labor Day Festival like when we were kids?"

Logan nodded. "This is the thirty-fifth year. Remember, you used to walk us into town because Mom and Dad wouldn't go? Somehow you always came up with the money so we could get cotton candy, hot dogs and have enough left over for a few rides."

Jake remembered. He'd spend all summer each year collecting soda-pop cans and pilfering change from his father's dresser to have money to show his siblings a good time at the festival. It was the one weekend they all looked forward to each year, when they could forget the troubles at home and simply have a good time. Other than the people he'd encountered at the hospital and locals at the bakery, Jake had managed to avoid running into many people who knew him back then. It was exactly the way he wanted it to remain.

"Brooke would love it," Olivia said, breaking his reverie.

"I'm sure she will." He nodded. "I'll talk to Millie."

He thought of his promise to go "all-in" on being a good parent. "Plan on seeing us there."

"Daddy, you need to wear the crown."

Millie smiled at the horrified expression that crossed Jake's face as Brooke climbed the back steps to the porch and placed the ring of dandelions on top of his head.

"You're the prince."

"Can I be the prince without wearing flowers in my hair?" He met Millie's gaze and grimaced.

She shook her head at the same time Brooke said, "You have to wear the crown."

Millie and Brooke had spent the past hour playing in the backyard, creating a kingdom of rock-and-log thrones, pretend soup and the flower crowns. It was the kind of play Millie had loved as a girl, when she'd spent most of her time in the small woods next to their condo during her father's visits. The condo wasn't large and her mother had always wanted privacy with her dad, leaving Millie to fend for herself outdoors. Neither of her parents had ever joined her on her imaginary adventures, so she'd been surprised when Jake had returned home from an afternoon spent with his brothers and come to sit on the patio steps, helping to stir mud-and-leaf stew for his daughter.

He adjusted the band of flowers. Somehow the whimsical crown didn't detract from his masculinity. In fact, the contrast somehow made him look even more appealing. As if he needed help in that area.

The doorbell sounded from inside the house.

"Pizza's here," Brooke announced.

"We didn't order pizza tonight," Millie told her. "Remember, we made lasagna after the museum today. It's in the oven."

"I'll see who it is," Jake said, standing but not removing the flowers from his hair. "Maybe I left something in Logan's car."

As he walked into the house, Millie lay back on the quilt she'd spread in the yard. She felt emotion uncurl in her stomach, a mix of happiness and hope she hadn't experienced in a long time. Being with Brooke gave her life a sort of gentle purpose she relished. It was odd to feel as if she belonged in this little girl's life. Her feelings for Jake were more complicated, but there was an underlying sense of rightness she couldn't deny. Even if it was only temporary, she planned to savor every moment she had in Crimson.

She closed her eyes as Brooke began to rain blades of grass down on her.

"It's a magic blanket," the girl told her. "When you fall asleep with this covering you, your dreams come true."

It had been so long since Millie had dared to dream, she didn't know how to respond. Instead, she enjoyed the warmth of the early-evening sun and the smell of fresh grass surrounding her. The tiny pieces of grass tickled her bare arms and legs, and she let herself relax in the moment.

After a few minutes Jake's voice broke her reverie. "Brooke, will you come up here?" His voice sounded different than it had a few minutes ago, tighter and more controlled. "I have a friend I'd like you to meet."

Millie sat up, blinking several times to shake the daydreams that had so quickly populated her brain. Dreams of love, a family and a place that would finally feel like home. As Brooke skipped over to the porch, Millie stood and dusted the grass off her denim shorts and the Life Is Sweet T-shirt Katie had given her when she and Brooke had made their now-daily stop to the bakery earlier.

Jake stood on the porch, a woman at his side whom

Millie didn't recognize. She couldn't have been a Crimson native. Everything about her, from her silk blouse to her pencil skirt and leather pumps, screamed "big city." Even though she'd grown up in DC, Millie had never fit that mold thanks to her mother's unconventional influence.

She quickly pulled down the hem of her shirt and tucked her hair behind her ear, groaning as more grass blades fell to the blanket around her. Tucking the blanket under her arms in front of her like a shield, she slowly made her way to the edge of the porch.

"Lana," Jake said, his hand on the base of the woman's back, "this is Millie Spencer, Brooke's nanny."

The woman gave Millie a long look up and down. Up close, she was stunning—with high cheekbones and glossy hair that was arranged in a sleek knot at the back of her neck. Millie noticed that the dandelion crown drooped in Jake's injured hand and she quickly pulled the flowers out of her hair.

"How sweet," Lana said, but her patronizing tone made Millie feel anything but sweet. "You have a daughter *and* a nanny." She put her hand on Jake's arm and squeezed, leaning closer. "We definitely have a lot to catch up on, Jake."

Lana bent over Brooke as if she was examining her, the tight smile still in place. "How old are you, honey?"

"Four," Brooke answered, holding Bunny in the telltale death grip that Millie had come to know meant the girl was nervous. Jake didn't seem to notice.

"Lana and I did our residency together," Jake told Millie. "She's a brilliant doctor and is finishing a fellowship at the clinic here in Crimson."

"Brilliant," Millie repeated. "That's nice." She was all too aware of her disheveled appearance and bare feet in comparison to Lana, who looked as if she'd just stepped out of a fashion magazine or boardroom, not a county hospital in the mountains of Colorado. No one in the world had ever described Millie as brilliant. As her mother always told her, the Spencers had other ways of attracting attention besides their brains. Millie had always wanted to be one of the smart ones, wishing she'd inherited more than her father's brown eyes.

"Lana brought dinner," Jake said with a slightly apologetic wave in Millie's direction.

"We made lasagna," Brooke told him. "Remember? I cut the cheese." She laughed at the joke she and Millie had shared earlier. Millie smiled along with her but noticed Lana's brows furrow.

She thought she saw one corner of Jake's mouth curve, but it was so quick she might have imagined it. "The lasagna will hold until tomorrow. Right, Millie?"

Her face burned but she nodded. "Sure."

"I don't know if I have enough for everyone." Lana's mouth turned into a perfect pout. "I picked up Chinese." Millie watched as the woman's chin dipped. "Kung pao chicken used to be your favorite, Jake. Do you remember all those takeout nights after our shifts?"

Millie wanted to gag as Jake stuttered. "I…uh…guess."

"I thought it would just be the two of us, but of course I want to include your daughter." She slid Millie a pointed look.

She might not be "brilliant," but Millie could take a hint. "I'll wrap up the lasagna for another time. You three can have dinner. I ate a big lunch, so I'm not that hungry."

"You had a salad," Brooke pointed out.

"It was a *big* salad."

Lana clapped her hands together, clearly having expected to get her way. "Perfect."

"I bet there'd be enough. Are you sure, Millie?" Jake's voice was so kind it made her throat tight.

She gave a jerky nod. "I'm going to clean up out here. Brooke, wash your hands before eating, okay?"

"Yep." With a quick glance at Millie, the girl ran back into the yard and plucked up the final crown of flowers. She returned and handed it to Lana. "You can be the dinner princess," she said with a smile.

Lana held the flowers gingerly in her hands. "Thanks," she said as if Brooke had handed her a wiggling snake.

"Let's go, Cookie." Jake scooped up Brooke and Bunny in one arm. "We don't want the food to get cold."

And with that Millie was left alone in the backyard. She couldn't be mad, she told herself, despite the ball of emotion lodged in her chest. Lana was a friend of Jake's. She'd been a colleague, someone he shared things in common with and could relate to on a meaningful level. She looked perfect next to him, like a doctor's wife should look. That woman could say whatever she wanted about catching up, but Millie recognized the look of possessiveness in her eyes. She'd been part of Jake's past, and from the looks of it, she had every intention of becoming part of his future.

Millie was a temporary fix. She was the nanny. The hired help. She was a placeholder, like she'd always been in life. That had been enough for her mother, but never for Millie. Her wishes didn't seem to matter. When it was time to have fun, make messes and take a break from life, Millie was the type of person you wanted around. When it was time for things to get real, she was left behind.

Just like always.

There were times Jake knew his life would be easier if he lived on a mountaintop in some remote part of the world where there weren't any women to be found for miles.

Tonight was one of those times.

He hadn't planned on Lana Mayfield showing up at the house with Chinese. Hell, he didn't even remember what he'd eaten most of his residency since the times he hadn't been at the hospital had passed in a blur. If she said he liked kung pao chicken, he wasn't going to argue. He hadn't understood that it might be a big deal to postpone the meal Millie and Brooke had made for another night.

Mistake number one.

He'd also assumed that when Millie had so quickly agreed that it would be best that she be left out of the dinner, it had meant she wanted time to herself. A night off. A break. He could certainly understand why she would want that.

Mistake number two.

Of course, he hadn't realized he'd made either of those mistakes until his sister-in-law Sara had called a few minutes ago.

Millie had remained in her room until they'd finished eating. Then she'd taken Brooke in to have a bath and get ready for bed. He'd gotten the distinct vibe Lana would have liked to stay longer, but he knew Brooke would want him to read her a bedtime story. Those quiet moments with his daughter had become the highlight of each day for him.

As he was heading back toward Brooke's bedroom after Lana left, he'd picked up Sara's call. She'd asked about the lasagna—apparently it had been a Crimson Ranch recipe—and when he'd explained the delay in eating it, he'd been greeted with a heavy silence on the other end of the line.

Not a good silence.

"I thought you were the smart brother," she said finally and proceeded to explain—in great detail—why his actions had been rude and probably hurtful to Millie. That hadn't been his intention and he wondered how he was going to fix it.

Only a short time ago, Jake had been able to fix any number of physical injuries and illness. Now he was at a loss.

He hoped Sara had been wrong in her assessment of the situation.

"Sorry if I messed up dinner plans," he said, blocking Millie's path out of Brooke's room.

"No big deal. I had some email to catch up on."

"So you enjoyed a little time to yourself?"

She leveled a look at him then flashed the brightest smile he'd ever seen. "It was peachy."

"You do so much with Brooke..." he said, trying another tactic.

"You pay me," she shot back immediately.

He took a breath. "Yes, but you don't have to be on call twenty-four hours. If you want a night off, I can handle things here."

"With Lana?" Her voice was icy cold.

Allowing Lana to stay for dinner was mistake number three, apparently.

"She's an old friend. Nothing more."

"You don't owe me an explanation." More frost.

He looked down at her, wanting to make this better but not having any idea how to accomplish that. She still smelled like the outdoors, fresh and clean and too damned appealing. He liked her bubbly and happy, but he found he liked her irritated, too. That was a big problem. A blade of grass still clung to her hair, and he loosened it from the soft strand, his body going tight at her quick intake of breath.

"I'm going to take a shower," she said. He had an immediate image of water pouring over her skin.

Mistake number four.

He nodded and let her walk past then took a deep, head-clearing breath before moving toward his daughter.

Thirty minutes later, he eased the door to Brooke's room closed. He could hear Millie in the kitchen and resolved that he would not make more of a mess of this evening than he already had.

She had her back to him, standing in front of the open freezer door.

"Looking for leftovers?" he asked as he came to stand at the edge of the room.

Obviously—he hoped—she hadn't heard him come into the room. She spun around and hurled her spoon at his head. It twirled in the air then hit him directly between the eyes.

"Ouch." He rubbed at the spot on his forehead and bent forward to retrieve the spoon.

Millie rushed toward him, their heads almost colliding. She grabbed on to his shoulders, pressing the front of her body against him as she tried to drag him toward the center island. For a moment he didn't resist, so overwhelmed by the feel of her soft curves and the scent of ripe berries and chocolate—a combination of her shampoo and ice cream, he guessed.

She tugged on him, but he stopped moving. "What are you doing, Millie?"

She wrenched at him again, not quite knocking him off balance. "I thought you were going to faint."

"From being dinged in the head with a teaspoon?" He grinned at the thought. Millie looked completely serious.

"How many fingers am I holding up?"

"Two."

"Do you have a headache?"

His head wasn't the part of his body with the ache at the moment.

"I'm fine. It hardly hurt. I was just picking up the spoon." He held it up for her to see. "Sorry I startled you."

"I thought you were with Brooke."

"She fell asleep."

Jake couldn't help but notice she hadn't moved away from him. He tried to remain as still as possible to prolong his pleasure in this moment.

His gaze flicked to the refrigerator. "What were you doing in the freezer?"

She bit down on her lower lip and looked away before answering, "Having dinner."

"Ice cream?"

She nodded.

"Why didn't you eat with us?"

"There wasn't enough food."

"Bull. We would have made it work."

She tried to pull away but he held her fast. "I spent enough of my life being the third wheel to my mom and dad. I wasn't going to be the fourth one tonight." Her voice held so much vulnerability and sadness, he almost couldn't stand it. "It's fine. Really. I work for you. We're not friends. We don't—"

"No." He cut her off, raising his hands to cup her face, forcing her to look him in the eye. "We *are* friends, Millie. Hell, you're one of the few I have in my life. I've never been great at making friends."

Her sweet lips pressed together. "Lana Mayfield and her trip-down-memory-lane Chinese would argue with that."

"Lana is great." He leaned in closer, just a breath away from her. "It was nice to see her. But she isn't…"

* * *

Millie waited for him to finish his sentence then got distracted looking into his blue eyes, which had gone several shades darker as he watched her.

"She isn't what?"

His mouth grazed hers ever so slightly, the light pressure making her ache for more.

"You," he whispered, the word humming against her skin. "She isn't you."

Millie sighed as he deepened the kiss, relishing the strength and warmth of him. The kiss was a revelation because as much power as she knew he possessed, he didn't wield it against her. He allowed her to lead, to explore him at her own pace. There was an intimate give and take as their tongues met and melded. Still he held back, reining in his need and stoking hers in a way she'd never before experienced.

It left her wanting more. She wound her arms around the back of his neck. Her fingers laced through the soft hair that curled at his collar, urging him closer. He took her silent invitation, enveloping her in his embrace.

The moments turned into minutes as they stood wound around each other.

"You feel so good." He released her mouth to press kisses along her jaw and then down her neck, nipping at her skin then soothing those heated spots with his tongue. His fingers touched her back underneath her pajama top and her whole body ached from the pleasure of it.

"More," she whispered and let her own hands snake under his T-shirt to the hard muscle of his back and torso.

They were a tangle of arms and legs as he claimed her mouth again. She felt her knees tremble and he steadied her with his injured hand, the fabric of his splint scratching against her exposed skin.

She felt her control slipping. She was about to lose herself in the moment. She wanted to lose herself to this man.

The thought was scary enough to have her wrench away, pressing her palms to the kitchen counter to steady herself.

For a few minutes the only sound was the hum of the refrigerator and her heavy breaths as she tried to regain control of herself. She stole a glance at Jake out of the corner of her eye. He watched her from hooded eyes, his arms loose at his sides. Although he looked totally in control, she could see his chest rise and fall in an unsteady rhythm. At least she wasn't alone in how much the kiss had affected her.

"I can't do this," she said faintly. She picked at a corner of the tile countertop. "It isn't right."

"It sure as hell felt right." She thought she heard condemnation in his tone, but maybe that was her own voice ringing in her head.

"I work for you, Jake."

"We're friends, Millie."

"Not that kind of friends."

Her mother had been her father's secretary when they'd first met. From the stories Millie had always heard, he'd swept her off her feet and left her mother unable to resist him. Millie had always promised herself that she would never lose sight of who she was. She would never allow a man to make her forget what she wanted from life.

She'd always thought of her mother as weak. But in this moment she understood how her dad had been able to capture her mother's heart in one moment and take command of her life for the next two decades. Because all she wanted was to wrap herself around Jake Travers and never let go. No matter if she wasn't good enough or smart enough. She didn't care about consequences or commitment. She'd always fought to remain in control of her emotions and her actions, but every time that resolve slipped Millie found herself in trouble.

Now she was standing on the edge of a yawning cavern, and she knew if she didn't pull herself away she'd be lost.

She could lose herself in Jake.

Hugging her arms around her body, she straightened and looked at him.

"I'm not going there… We can't go there."

"What's wrong, Millie?" His gaze pinned her in place. "What happened to you to make you so scared?"

She took a breath. "I'm not scared. I called the preschool. I'm interviewing with Laura tomorrow. If things work out, I'll start the Tuesday after Labor Day, the same hours as Brooke so I'll still be able to take care of her."

"Okay, good. I think you'll be perfect for that." He shifted. "I meant what I said, Millie. You're not on call twenty-four hours here. If there are other things you want to do or you need time off—whether for a job or something else—we'll make that work."

"I'll take you up on that."

How else was she supposed to answer? *No, thanks. I don't have a life or friends or any hobbies. The only time I feel remotely content is when I'm with you and your daughter. That's how pathetic I am.*

No, she wouldn't admit any of that. Instead, she'd walk away.

As hard as it was. As much as it hurt. Because walking away had always been easier than staying and fighting for things she didn't believe she deserved.

“And that’s all?” His voice pierced her thoughts.

“That’s all,” she agreed then turned and fled back to the safety of her bedroom.

Chapter Nine

Millie popped a chip into her mouth and took a long sip from her margarita.

"Nothing cures what's ailing you quite like tequila," Natalie said and poked her gently in the ribs.

"I wish it were that easy." Millie scooped more salsa onto a chip.

She'd met Natalie, Olivia and Katie at the local Mexican restaurant for a girls' dinner. Sara had flown to California for a night to attend some fancy Hollywood party, so she was the only one missing from the group of friends.

Friends.

Millie rolled the word over in her mind, liking the sound of it. Usually she dealt with issues privately, or she called her mother. Her mom wasn't much on listening, but she always had enough going on to distract Millie from her own problems.

When Olivia had called earlier, Millie hadn't meant to

share everything, from Brooke's grandparents arriving early to Jake's none-too-subtle suggestion that she get a life of her own. But it had all come spilling out. To her surprise, Olivia had immediately suggested that a girls' night out was just what Millie needed.

Jake had seemed shocked that Millie was actually leaving for the night. As shocked as Millie that the women she was getting to know in Crimson would make time for her.

But they were here, and Millie felt the comforting arms of new friendship wrap around her. She blinked against the tears that pricked at the backs of her eyes.

"Too spicy?" Katie asked from across the table, a knowing look in her green eyes.

"Something like that."

"So tell us all about Dr. Easy-On-The-Eyes and the trouble he's causing." Natalie nudged her again.

"No trouble," Millie said quickly. "I love being with Brooke, and Jake's very helpful in his own way."

"For a guy who doesn't know the first thing about being a father," Olivia suggested.

"Exactly."

"And when he kissed you…" Natalie prompted.

"It was…" Millie broke off, realizing that she hadn't mentioned their kiss to anyone, not even her sister. Mortified, she thumped the palm of her hand against her head. "It was nothing. It didn't happen. I'm a total idiot."

"There's no use denying anything with Natalie," Olivia told her. "She's like a mind reader." She shook a chip at Natalie. "Your time will come and we'll all be here to witness it."

"Oh, no," Natalie argued. "My time has come and gone. I want nothing to do with men. Been there, done that. Got the amazing kid to prove it. Back to you, Millie."

"It was really nothing. Less than…"

"A kiss from Jake Travers is less than nothing?"

The food was delivered to the table at that moment, allowing Millie to collect her thoughts before answering. "It was lovely, as you might imagine."

"Lovely," Katie repeated with a sigh.

Natalie snorted. Olivia smiled across the table.

"It meant nothing and we agreed it wouldn't…couldn't happen again. I work for him. His priority is Brooke."

"Doesn't stop either of you from being human," Natalie commented as she forked up a bite of taco salad.

"It stops me from acting on it." Millie picked up her fish taco.

"Logan and Josh want him to stay in Crimson, even after he's fully recovered." Olivia's gaze was kind. "You could stay here, too."

"It's a wonderful place," Millie agreed, "but I don't want to impose on your life any more than I already have."

"You're my sister, not an imposition."

"And Jake isn't…"

"You like him?" Olivia formed the words as a question, but Millie knew her feelings were obvious to each of these women.

"He's not for me." She wiped her fingers on her napkin. "There's a woman working at the hospital he knew from his residency. I think they dated or something. She brought dinner over the other night."

"Competition. Nice." Natalie tapped her fork on her plate. "What's she like, this harpy who's after your man?"

Millie nearly choked on her taco. "She's a doctor—smart, beautiful and totally different from me. But he's not my man. She's not competition. It isn't—"

"Just know we've got your back if you ever need it," Natalie said.

The words brought another wave of emotion cresting in Millie's chest. No one ever had her back. "I'm not looking for a relationship."

Olivia tilted her head. "But if the right person comes along, it's a shame to ignore it."

"Olivia tried to ignore Logan," Natalie said. "We were witnesses."

"Whatever happens," Katie offered, "it's nice that Jake has you in his life right now. I never imagined him as a father, so having someone to help ease this transition has to be a big deal for him."

Easing the transition. That was exactly what she was doing. Nothing more. But as she laughed and talked with these women, Millie realized how much she wanted to have a life that included friends and a community like Crimson. It was difficult to miss something you'd never had. Now that she'd experienced this kind of support, how could she go back to her solitary life?

Brooke's grandparents arrived two days early. It shouldn't have surprised Jake. He was fairly certain they were trying to catch him unaware, probably hoping to find Brooke and him living in chaotic squalor filled with empty pizza boxes and dirty clothes.

That might have been the case if it hadn't been for Millie. He hadn't lied when he told Olivia that her sister was the most ruthlessly organized person he knew. Millie's demeanor might be all rainbows and sunshine but she ran the house with the precision of a military sergeant.

Thanks to that, Janis and John Smith seemed shocked to find Brooke happily ensconced in a homemade Play-Doh project at the kitchen table.

Her hair was done up in one of the intricate braids that she begged Millie for each morning. Her ballet getup was clean, her face scrubbed after lunch, and she hummed along with the kids' channel playing from the speakers attached to the computer.

She took the arrival of her grandparents in typical stride. "Nana, Papa, do you want some pizza?" she asked, holding up her colorful creation.

Janis dabbed at her eyes. "Oh, sweetie, I've missed you so much. Come over here and give your nana a kiss."

Brooke dutifully got up from the table and dusted off her palms. She let Janis wrap her in a tight embrace then gave John a hug, as well.

The front door opened at that moment. He heard Millie's voice. "I brought cookies from Life Is Sweet."

Jake watched as she stopped in the middle of the family room.

"Brooke's grandparents are here," he told her as if that wasn't obvious.

"Fairy Poppins is home," Brooke told her grandparents. "She's my nanny. She's nice and she likes blueberry muffins the best."

"A nanny?" One of Janis's brows rose. "Is that really necessary?"

"I'm in the leg brace for at least another week, Janis. I can't drive, and I have to get to my appointments. What would you propose as an alternative?"

"I thought you came to Crimson because your family is here. Can't they help you?"

He wasn't going to explain that he didn't want or deserve his brothers' help. "This works best."

She shook her head. "Stacy was a hands-on mother."

"Stacy traveled quite a lot for her work," Jake argued. "She told me as much."

"She had us," Janis countered.

"And a good day care so if—"

"Stop." Millie's voice interrupted their argument. "This isn't helping."

Jake's gaze moved to his daughter, who had inched her way over to the table to grab Bunny. He knew what that meant.

"The nanny's right," John said. He held out his hand. "I'm Brooke's grandfather, John Smith. I'd guess you don't always go by Fairy Poppins."

"Millie Spencer." Millie shook John's hand, giving him a sweet smile. "I'm so sorry for your loss, but I'm happy to meet you both. Brooke should be surrounded with all the people who love her."

"My point exactly." Janis sniffed. "Which is why we want her back in Atlanta, where she can be with family."

"She has family in Crimson, too." Jake knew he was being baited but couldn't seem to help his response.

"Where are they?" Janis hitched her chin as if making an important point. "Why is she being cared for by a s-t-r-a-n-g-e-r?" She spelled the final word.

Jake wanted to growl with frustration. "She's being cared for by me. Her father. The way Stacy wanted."

Millie stepped forward. "My sister is married to Jake's youngest brother, Logan," she said, gently leading Brooke back to the table. "I'm in town for a few months and I have experience working with children, so I offered to help Jake for a bit. His family *is* involved. I know he wants both of you to be involved, as well." She gave him a pointed look.

"That's true. I don't want to make things more difficult for Brooke." He took a breath then continued, "I'm glad you're here, Janis. We need to make an effort with each other. It's the only way this is going to work."

Janis didn't look convinced, but John took her arm.

"Have a piece of your granddaughter's pizza, hon." Millie moved out a chair so Janis could sit next to Brooke.

"Can Nana have a cookie?"

"Of course," Millie answered. "Can I get either of you something to drink?"

"A glass of water, I suppose. I bake my cookies from scratch, but I'll try a bite of one if it makes you happy, sweetie."

"I bake cookies, Nana." Brooke spread her arms wide. "Katie—she owns the bakery—has a mixer this big that I can use. Millie makes her pancakes and Frenchy toast from scratch. Daddy can only do eggs."

Janis sniffed then began to roll tiny pieces of Play-Doh between her fingers. "Your mother spent hours as a girl making Play-Doh creations. Remember how many colors we have back at Nana and Papa's house?" She refused to make eye contact with Jake.

John tipped his head toward the front of the house and Jake followed the older man to the office. "This is difficult for Janis," John said once they were out of earshot.

"It's hard for all of us." Jake wasn't feeling particularly sympathetic at the moment.

"That little girl is all we have left of our daughter."

The anger went out of Jake like a deflated balloon. Of course these two people were hurting. By all accounts, Stacy's parents were wonderful people. They'd been devastated by their daughter's death. Then Jake had come in and taken their granddaughter from them. "I'm sorry, John. I don't want to hurt you and Janis." He ran a hand through his hair. "I'm doing my best to honor Stacy's wishes."

"When this all started, you agreed it would be best for Brooke to live with us in Georgia."

A dull ache settled in Jake's chest. "I want to get to

know my daughter. Even if… When she comes to live with you, I will still be a part of her life."

The older man nodded slowly. "I'm glad to hear you say that, son. I wasn't sure you felt that way when we first met."

"It was a lot to digest." Jake didn't try to mask the bitterness in his voice.

"I loved my daughter." John's voice broke off and he cleared his throat then continued, "She was the best part of our lives. Janis and I still can't believe she's gone. But I never agreed with her keeping Brooke a secret from you. I know she had her reasons, but that doesn't make it right."

"She had her reasons," Jake repeated. Stacy had practically spit them at him the night he'd found out about Brooke. Everything had centered on her belief that he was unable to commit, that he wouldn't make the changes she thought necessary to be a true father to his daughter. "Then why, John? Why did she find me like she did? Why did she ask me to take care of Brooke with her last breath? What changed? Why now?"

"I don't know. I wish I did. Janis and I were shocked when she left to go to you. She wouldn't talk about it, only told us it was best for Brooke. Her first priority was always Brooke. Ours is, too. You have to know that Janis only means well."

"But she doesn't believe that I do? What happens if I share custody with you? Is Janis going to let me be involved?"

"Will you want to be involved?" He pointed to Jake's arm. "If you're able to take up where you left off with your agency, how involved will you really be? I know you're doing your best here, Jake. Is that enough?"

He'd thought the same thing only weeks ago. His plan

had been to come to Crimson, fulfill a mother's dying wish that he get to know his daughter, then move on from there. As cold as it sounded, getting to know Brooke had been one more thing to check off his list. One thing to fill the time while his body healed before he returned to regular life. No wonder Janis seemed so shocked at his attitude now.

Something had changed in him. His feelings for his daughter had changed him. And Millie. Her belief that he could become a decent father was a powerful influence on his intentions. He wanted to believe she was right.

"You can't believe it's best for Brooke to have her grandmother and her father at odds. Janis isn't going to listen to me, but you have to convince her that we need peace between us. For Brooke's sake."

John nodded. "I'll do my best."

"That's all any of us can do." Jake held out hope that his best would be good enough.

The Labor Day Festival was in full swing by the time Jake, Millie and Brooke caught up with Jake's brothers and their wives. They were seated at two tables set up off to the side of the main food-tent area. The sun had just ducked behind the mountain peak, leaving the evening light tinged in a soft shade of pink. Millie loved the energy of the event.

Residents laughed and talked, greeting each other by name under the glow of hanging lights while families in town for vacation appeared to soak up the gold rush–themed activities. Millie held the bag of gems and "fool's gold" Brooke had panned for earlier and tipped back the straw cowboy hat Jake had bought for both her and Brooke at one of the booths. A bluegrass trio played from the stage nearby, the music filling the air along with the scents of carnival food. An older couple danced together in front of the stage, and Millie wondered if she'd ever experienced a more perfect night.

"I love cotton candy," Brooke announced to the group, licking her fingers. The spun sugar seemed to be a four-year-old version of perfection.

"You polished that off in record time," Jake said as he dipped the corner of a napkin into his water cup. "But no more sweets or you'll end up with a tummy ache tonight." He gently wiped the napkin across Brooke's cheek, cleaning off a spot of dried cotton candy.

Millie's heart swelled at his unconscious movements and the way he smiled at his daughter as he worked.

"Except maybe a funnel cake," Brooke said, her tone serious. "Uncle Josh said I haven't lived until I tried a funnel cake. I want to live."

Jake threw a look to his brother who shrugged. "At least she gets her sweet tooth honestly," Josh offered. "It's a Travers tradition."

"Remember the year Beth was sick all the way home?" Logan laughed. "That girl loved candy like no other."

Brooke tugged on Jake's plaid shirt. "Who's Beth, Daddy?"

All eyes went to Jake. "She was my sister, sweetie. Your uncle Logan's twin. But she died when she was in high school. It was very sad for all of us."

Brooke gave him a knowing smile. "It's sad when someone dies. But maybe Aunt Beth is friends with Mommy in heaven."

Millie thought it was a testament to how far Jake had come in his relationship with Brooke that he didn't look shocked at her observation. "I bet they are good friends, Cookie," he answered.

Logan gave Olivia's shoulder a gentle squeeze, making Millie's heart melt a tiny bit. He took his wife's hand in his, kissed her knuckles and stood. "Let's go track down the funnel-cake booth, Brooke. I could use more dessert myself."

"We'll come, too," Josh said, wrapping his arm around Sara's waist. "Claire is here with a group of friends and I want to make sure she's okay."

"You mean you want to stare down any boy who comes within twenty feet of her," Sara said with a laugh.

"That, too," he agreed then turned to Jake and Millie. "We'll be back in a bit. Do you two need anything?"

Millie shook her head.

"I'll bring you some funnel cake," Brooke promised.

"Have fun, sweetie." Jake pointed a finger at his two brothers. "One funnel cake and that's the end of her sweets for the night."

"Spoken like a true parent." Logan swung Brooke onto his shoulders while she laughed, turning to wave to Jake and Millie as the group walked away.

"This has been a wonderful evening," Millie said when they were alone at the table. "Thanks for including me in it."

"The Labor Day celebration is a big deal in Crimson. Always has been." After a moment he reached across the table and laced his fingers with hers. "I'm glad you're here, Millie. I couldn't imagine doing any of this without you."

She didn't know how to respond without revealing how quickly her feelings for him had grown. They sat in a comfortable silence for several minutes, listening to the band and people watching. A group of kids, clearly siblings, walked by them, herded by an older brother who was trying to keep his young charges under control. She saw Jake's mouth harden into a thin line as they passed.

"You had a lot of responsibility for your brothers and sister," she said softly.

"Someone had to," he answered, not meeting her gaze. "I could have done better."

When he started to pull his hand away from hers, she tightened her grip.

"Josh and Logan love you," she told him. "They don't hold you responsible for the fact that you all had a crummy family life. You were just a kid, too."

"I was the oldest."

"But still a boy. You helped out the best you could. Children aren't supposed to raise each other." She gave a gentle tug on his hand and smiled, trying to lighten the mood. "I'm sure you read *Lord of the Flies* in school. You know leaving kids in charge doesn't work."

To her relief, he let out a small chuckle. "Well, we weren't quite stranded on a deserted island, but I appreciate your point."

He lifted their hands, turned them over and placed a soft kiss on the inside of her wrist. "You make me smile, Millie. Thank you." His touch left shivers across her skin. Millie felt herself leaning closer to him. He tucked a loose strand of hair behind her ear and trailed one finger along her jaw. "I want to kiss you again," he whispered.

Desire pooled low in her belly at his words. *Let's get on with it,* her body practically screamed. But she shook her head. "Not here. Brooke and the others could come back at any moment."

Jake let out a breath. "Maybe not here," he agreed, "but just know that I want to kiss you." He flashed her a rakish grin. "A lot."

The way his voice went a little hoarse on those last words made her whole body tingle. She had half a mind to pull him out of the chair and hide behind one of the nearby booths for a chance to make out like teenagers. Before the thought had fully formed in her head, Brooke came running back to the table.

"I brought funnel cake," she squealed, thrusting a wax-paper package toward them.

Millie dropped Jake's hand and wiped a bit of powdered sugar from the girl's cheek. "I can't wait."

She glanced up at Jake, and he gave her a small wink. She realized her words could refer to more than just the carnival dessert and felt a blush creep into her cheeks.

She was way in over her head here and took a big bite of funnel cake, trying to tamp down her feelings as she swallowed the sweet, doughy dessert. Millie wasn't worried about getting a stomachache, but her heart was another matter.

Chapter Ten

Jake woke in the middle of the night later that week, drenched in sweat, his heart pounding. Another nightmare. He rubbed his hands over his eyes and sat up on the edge of the bed until he could get his breathing under control.

The doctor had given him sleeping pills, but he hated taking them, afraid he'd miss something if Brooke needed him. But all his attempts to grit his way through the nights were failing miserably.

The dreams didn't come every night, but when they did he was a prisoner to them, reliving the last few minutes of Stacy's life, the deafening roar of the building's foundation giving way and the mad tremble of the ground under his feet.

He heard a sound from outside his bedroom and noticed a faint light shining under the closed door. He'd woken Brooke once before yelling out in his sleep and hoped his daughter was still tucked away in her bed. The last thing he wanted to do was scare her. His leg protested at the speed with which he made it across the hall. But instead of Brooke asleep, he found Millie holding her close as the two slowly swayed around the room, Millie singing softly in her beautiful voice.

Her eyes widened slightly as he came into the room, darting down then up his body before remaining glued to his face. Jake realized he was wearing only boxers and started to turn to put on a shirt.

Brooke lifted her head at that moment. “Daddy,” she said, her voice still drowsy with sleep, “you had a baddy dream.”

“I did, sweetie.” He walked toward her when she reached for him. “I’m sorry I woke you.”

“Millie was singing me back to sleep.” He went to lift Brooke out of Millie’s arms, but his daughter latched her arm around his neck and pulled him close. “She can sing for you, too.”

Their three heads were close together now and it was almost impossible to keep from touching Millie as Brooke remained in her arms. He could feel Millie’s warmth, smell the flowery scent of her shampoo. His nanny looked impossibly beautiful and sweet in the soft glow of Brooke’s night-light.

She’d come home earlier, her eyes gleaming with happiness, from another dinner out with friends. She’d been almost buzzing with excitement, as if actually having fun with a group of girlfriends made her happy in a way she hadn’t felt before. He liked her like that, he’d realized, and had told himself that he was going to put more fun back into both of their lives.

“Your daddy will put you to bed again,” Millie said, extracting herself from the embrace. Jake saw her chest rise and fall and wondered if her heart was beating at the same annoyingly frantic pace as his.

"I need to go potty first." Brooke squirmed in his arms.

She headed toward the bathroom in the hall, leaving Jake and Millie alone in the room. The intimacy of the moment crashed through him. He shouldn't be aware of this woman the way he was. He shouldn't want her like he did but couldn't seem to stop himself.

"Doesn't right now prove this isn't going to work?" He ran his hands through his hair.

"What are you talking about?" Her voice sounded hoarse and she took a step back. She wore another pair of cotton pajama pants and a thin tank top.

"She woke up because of my nightmare."

Millie gave a gentle nod. "She wanted to go to you, but I wasn't sure if that was a good idea."

"Because I might lash out in my sleep?"

"I know you wouldn't hurt her."

"You don't know that. Hell, I don't know that. My daughter can't even sleep through the night because I wake her up with my yelling."

"Things take time to settle, Jake."

"What if they don't? What if I can't settle?" He broke off, hating the tremble in his voice. That was his biggest fear, that he couldn't do this. That he'd fail. He didn't want to fail Brooke, but for all the things he was getting right, did it really matter? What if he was truly like his father, unable to do the right thing when it counted?

Millie came forward now, her eyes intent on his. He expected her to walk past him, but she slid her arms around his neck. Her fingers threaded through his hair as she pulled his head down to hers. But she didn't kiss him. Her lips touched his ear, grazing the soft skin there.

"Breathe, Jake," she whispered. "Take a deep breath."

He did. His hands wound around her waist, pulling her against him, and he buried his face in her softness, taking in her scent. In and out until his breathing calmed.

Still she held him, nothing more. And he let her. It had been so long since he'd derived comfort from someone in this way, his knees went weak with it. He'd stood on his own, by himself, for as long as he could remember. But now this tiny pixie of a woman drove away his late-night demons with the light that radiated from her core. How did she know that this was exactly what he needed, when he didn't even realize it himself?

"I believe in you," she said softly after a moment. "I believe you can make this right."

His chest constricted at those words. He was used to proving himself. He'd made a career of working medical miracles in remote jungles and war-torn villages. But she gave him the gift of her faith without asking him to do a thing to earn it except stay. Try.

How could he deny her?

She broke away as Brooke returned to the room. His skin burned from where she'd been pressed against him and he felt the loss of her touch like a physical blow.

"Good night again, Brookie-Cookie." Millie bent and kissed the top of the girl's head. "Sweet dreams to you both."

As Brooke placed her hand in his, Millie left without another word.

Things were quiet in the house the next morning when Millie got out of bed. She took an extra long shower to try to make herself feel normal, thanks to that 2:00 a.m. interlude, which had left her dizzy with emotions.

But as much as she wanted Jake Travers, he needed her to keep her focus. He would make a wonderful father if he could only get past his doubts. That was where she came in, not for anything else.

She tiptoed down the hall to Brooke's bedroom, since the girl got up at the same time each day. Today was the first morning of preschool and she didn't want Brooke to feel rushed. Millie's hand shot to her mouth to cover her sharp intake of breath at the scene in front of her.

Apparently, Jake had remained in his daughter's bedroom last night. He was asleep on one side of the bed, most of his body near the edge as Brooke lay with her feet pushed into his side, diagonal on the bed. The girl had all the covers tucked around her, leaving Jake ever so visible.

Millie took in the slivered scar on his shoulder along with his lean, rangy muscles. He shifted and she jumped back, not wanting to be caught staring at him this way.

She made her way back to the kitchen thinking that if he had stayed all night with Brooke, maybe some of her confidence in his parenting abilities had rubbed off on him. She used to love to sneak into bed with her mother and feel not so alone in the world. Her mom had encouraged it and they'd spent many Saturday mornings curled up in bed watching cartoons. But when her father visited, there had been a strict no-access policy to her mother's bedroom. It had never seemed fair to Millie that she be the one to be cast off so easily when it was her father who made her mother cry when he left.

By the time she'd toasted bagels and cut up fruit for breakfast, Jake and Brooke were sliding into chairs at the kitchen table.

"Morning, you two sleepyheads." She put plates down in front of each of them.

"Hi, Millie," Brooke said cheerfully. "After you left, Daddy tucked me in." She giggled. "Then he fell asleep in my bed. And then I took all the covers and pushed him off the side."

"Twice," Jake clarified. To her relief—and disappointment—Jake had put on a T-shirt so his impressive body was covered.

Brooke scrambled off her chair. "I forgot Bunny. He's still sleeping." She ran back toward her bedroom.

"Thank you for last night." Jake gave her a slow smile. "I know it's above and beyond what you signed up for with this job."

"No worries," she said quickly. She still had trouble making eye contact with him as her mind kept drifting back to the image of him on the edge of the bed, his features gentled in sleep. His hair was still bed tousled and his cheeks held a shadow of stubble that appealed to her way too much.

"I get the brace off my ankle today," he said, unaware of the effect he was having on her. "You won't have to cart me around anymore."

"I don't mind." She turned to the sink, trying to get a grip on her rioting hormones before she made a fool of herself.

Apparently he took her short answers as anger over the previous night. "Millie, I'm sorry about last night. You made a huge difference to me and I—"

The end of his sentence was cut short when the doorbell rang.

"Nana and Papa are here," Brooke sang out as she barreled down the hall and around the corner, Bunny tucked under her arm.

"That can't be." Millie checked the clock on the oven. "It's barely eight o'clock. They were going to take her out for ice cream after preschool today but…"

Janis Smith bustled into the kitchen. "Hope you don't

mind," she said as she took in Jake at the table with Millie standing before him. "We wanted to see Brooke off to her first day of school." Her lips pursed into a thin line. "It seems like you're getting a late start, Jake. Stacy was always an early bird and made sure Brooke was dressed and ready to go with time to spare."

"There's plenty of time," Millie said between her teeth.

She saw John Smith shoot Jake an apologetic look.

"Daddy's tired because I pushed him off the bed." Brooke grinned as she climbed back into her seat and took a bite of banana.

"Why weren't you sleeping in your own bed?" Janis's tone was light but laced with disapproval.

"Daddy was in *my* bed," Brooke told her.

Millie thought the woman would faint dead away.

Before she could respond, Brooke continued, "He has bad dreams about Mommy dying and wakes up at night. But she's in heaven, so it's okay. And I helped him feel better. Even when I took all the covers." She spoke around a big bite of bagel.

No one said a word and Millie figured they were all as speechless as she was. Janis Smith had gone still as stone. Tears shimmered in the older woman's eyes.

"I'm going to get dressed," Brooke said as she finished the rest of her bagel. "Millie, will you braid my hair?"

"Of course, Cookie." She picked up Brooke's plate from the table. "Your nana can help you pick out an outfit. Then I'll come back to do your hair."

She placed a hand on Janis's arm. "Would you help her, please?"

The touch seemed to shake the woman out of her shock. "I'd love to. Let's go, Brooke."

"I'm sorry," Jake said to John as Janis and Brooke left the room. "I know it upsets Janis to talk about Stacy."

John shook his head, wiping at the corner of one eye. "This is hard on all of us, son. I left the camera in the car. I'll just go get it now."

When he was gone, Jake stood from the table. "I let their only daughter die."

"Jake," Millie whispered, "it wasn't your fault. You know that. They know that."

He only shook his head. "I'm going to shower. We're walking her to preschool, right?"

Millie nodded. "Unless you think it's too much on your leg."

"I can do it, Millie."

She forced a bright smile on her face. "I never doubted you."

Chapter Eleven

Millie might have faith in him, but Jake had enough doubts swirling around his mind for both of them. He couldn't believe how hard it was to leave Brooke at the preschool.

Not for her, of course. His social-butterfly daughter had marched into the preschool as if it was her long-lost home. He felt a huge knot clamp down on his stomach. Janis was audibly sniffing next to him.

"It's sometimes more difficult for the parents," Laura Wilkes said from the doorway where she watched the children gather on the rug.

"And grandparents," Janis said with a loud snuffle. John had chosen to wait outside, smart man.

Millie, who was also starting her first day as a teacher's aide, was sitting in a rocking chair near one side of the brightly colored rug. She leaned forward to speak to one of the boys, gently patting his head as he gazed up at her and sidled closer. Jake could understand the boy's desire to get closer to Millie. Jake had the same reaction. Something about her very presence soothed him. Now he'd have the whole morning to himself, not a prospect he found appealing.

"Do I just leave them—I mean her—here?"

Laura smiled. "That's the idea. She'll be fine, Dr. Travers." She leaned closer. "They both will."

Another family came into the front hall of the preschool at that point, and Jake backed away, tugging Janis with him. He adjusted his sunglasses as they walked into the morning sun.

"She's a wonderful little girl," Janis said.

"Yes, she is."

"Just like her mother."

"Come along, Janis." John held out a hand. "We'll see her in a few hours." He looked at Jake. "Are you walking back to the house?"

"You two go on. My brother's working on a house a few blocks from here, so I'm going to head there. He's giving me a ride to the hospital this morning."

"We could do that," John offered even as Janis stiffened.

"It's fine. Thanks."

Jake stood in front of the preschool for several more minutes. A few parents walked in and out as he watched. All of the children going in seemed happy to be there, which was a good indication that Brooke would love it, as well. He knew his daughter was adaptable to almost any situation. Look at how quickly she'd bonded with him, after all. He heard the murmur of young voices and then laughter spilled out from the classroom.

He had no idea it would be so difficult to be away from Brooke like this. Now he had a better understanding of how she'd felt when he'd gone to his physical-therapy appointments. He felt something at his feet and looked down to see an enormous cat winding its way through his legs.

"You get left behind, too, sweetheart?" He bent and scratched the cat behind the ears, rewarded by the sound of loud purring. "I've got nothing to offer you. Go on, then." The cat patently ignored him, much like both Millie and Brooke when he argued for televised sports during their nightly allotment of screen time. She continued to nuzzle him, especially enjoying the edge of his orthopedic boot. He let the quiet purr and the softness of her fur relax him until he felt able to leave the front yard of the preschool building.

Walking along the quiet streets of Crimson made him think about growing up in this town and how much he'd wanted to escape. For years Jake couldn't separate emotions about his childhood from the way he felt about Crimson. They seemed tied inexorably together. Now he realized the town hadn't been responsible for his miserable family life. The fact that both of his brothers could be so happy here was proof of that.

He saw Crimson now for what it was—a picturesque small mountain town filled with good, decent people. Everyone he'd met at the hospital, especially those who had recognized his name, had been friendly and supportive. Most had actually seemed proud of his accomplishments, as if his success reflected well on the town as a whole. As if they'd expected him to succeed in life.

What a novel concept.

Logan was unloading cabinets from the back of his truck as Jake walked up.

"How was the first day?" his brother asked, peering at him from underneath a Broncos ball cap.

"She's like Beth was as a girl—fearless and totally

confident." Until the words popped out of his mouth, Jake hadn't remembered that about his baby sister. But now he smiled at the memories of Beth running roughshod over all three of her brothers.

"In that case, you're in big trouble." Logan shook his head but laughed. Jake knew Logan had adored his twin sister.

"I'm sorry I didn't come back when you needed me. I should never have left you all with him. Then Josh took off with the rodeo tour, and you were even more alone."

"I don't blame you, Jake. Or Josh."

Jake thought back to Logan's anger after Beth's death. "You did back then."

"I blamed everyone back then." Logan handed him a toolbox. "Carry this to the house for me."

He hefted the oversize toolbox under his good arm.

"I blamed myself most of all," Logan told him as he pulled two large pieces of trim wood out of the back of the truck. "I learned that living in the past doesn't do much to help with the future."

"Your wife teach you that?"

"Among other things," Logan said with a wink.

Jake held the door open and Logan maneuvered through.

"I'm proud of you," Jake said, setting the toolbox on the counter.

Logan stilled. "What makes you say that?"

"It should have been said years ago. I wish we'd had the sort of parents to tell you—to tell any of us—something positive. I know Mom tried with you but not hard enough. You had a rough go of it early on, Logan. You came through that and you've got a good life."

"I remember how he used to go after you," Logan said after a moment. "I could never figure it out. Josh and I were the wild ones, always making noise and trouble.

But you took the brunt of his anger when he was drinking. I still don't understand why."

"He wanted to break me," Jake answered quietly. "He said I thought I was better than him. I got good grades and had a future. Maybe it was because he'd wasted his own chances, and the way we looked alike reminded him of that."

"It wasn't fair."

"He wasn't fair to anyone. But the three of us made it through. Every day I wish Beth had, too."

Logan watched him for several moments then nodded. "What time is your appointment today?"

"In about an hour."

"Great." Logan came over to the toolbox and pulled out a hammer. "You can help until then."

Jake held up his splint arm. "Are you sure that's a good idea?"

"I trust you, bro."

Jake took the hammer, his own heart pounding in his chest. "Let's get to work."

"Admit it, you really do like driving a big car."

Millie patted the front hood of her yellow Beetle. Josh had it waiting out in front at the ranch for her, washed and ready to go.

She'd known Jake was getting his leg brace off today, which would make him able to drive, but it had still been a bit of a shock to see him behind the wheel. Somehow driving him around had given her a sense of being needed. She knew he still needed help, but somehow the balance of power had shifted in her mind.

He'd been waiting at the end of the school day, and Brooke had raced into his arms. Even Janis couldn't deny Brooke's unwavering affection for her father. The girl had been reluctant to leave for ice cream and a movie with her grandparents, and Jake hadn't seemed to want to let her go. But he'd given her a hug and gently persuaded her what fun the afternoon would be with Janis and John. She'd seen John silently mouth "thank you" to him as the trio walked away.

Millie was exhausted after her first day helping to teach the group of two dozen preschoolers. She was contracted to work only the first two hours of the day but had found she didn't want to leave when her shift was through. Tired as she might be, she figured she'd had almost as much fun as Brooke over the course of the morning. The kids were energetic and sometimes needy, but Millie loved interacting with them. Laura Wilkes was gentle in her teaching, treating each child as an individual—just the sort of teaching mentor Millie had always wanted.

It was so different from the university internship that had ended so badly. Millie had needed to stop several times that morning to get control over her wayward emotions. She'd believed she was at fault for how things had gone at her previous school, but working with Laura for just a day had done wonders for her battered confidence.

After Brooke and the Smiths had gone, she and Jake had driven to Crimson Ranch for her car. "I like looking down on people," she told him with a smile. "But Bugsy is my one true love."

"Bugsy? You named your car?"

"Of course." She bent and gave the front glass a small kiss. "This car has been across the country twice, with me through a half dozen moves, a couple of university transfers and countless dead-end jobs. Up until I got to Crimson, Bugsy was the best friend I ever had."

"You kissed your car," he said, his voice dazed. "I don't understand you one bit, Fairy Poppins."

"Don't you have one thing that's seen you through all your trials and tribulations?"

He shook his head. "Not one thing."

"You do now."

His eyes darkened and she quickly clarified, "Brooke. You have your daughter."

"For now," he agreed.

"Forever," she countered.

His gaze rose to look past her to the mountains. The hills were still covered in green, with just a few splashes of the yellow that would soon dot the hillside as the aspens turned color in the fall. She knew autumn came early at this altitude. Already the temperature dropped almost ten degrees each evening before warming again during the day.

"Want to go for a walk?"

His question surprised her. "Where to?"

"Down by the river." He pointed. "Josh, Sara and everyone on the ranch are busy with guests. Brooke and the Smiths won't be back from the movie for another hour."

"Your leg is up to it?"

He nodded. "I need to exercise it more now that the boot is off to regain my strength."

Watching Jake in his fitted T-shirt and cargo shorts, she couldn't imagine him becoming much stronger. His body was so different from hers and she had to admit she appreciated him physically.

She started walking, not liking the turn her thoughts were taking. He outpaced her easily with his long strides, but they fell into an easy rhythm, matching their steps as they made their way down the path that wound through the ranch's back property. She loved the smell of the wild grasses mixed with the pine trees that flanked the trail.

As they approached the river, the sound of gurgling

water grew louder. She'd never been much of a mountain girl, but Millie was learning to love the wildness of the terrain surrounding Crimson. A rabbit darted out from a low bush near the river's edge.

"We used to hunt those as kids."

"You killed rabbits?"

He grinned at her. "I never tried very hard, but that's what you did to keep busy out where we lived. Josh was a better shot."

"Don't let Brooke hear you talk about killing bunnies. She'll be scarred for life."

"I'm pretty sure I've already accomplished that." He picked up a flat rock and skipped it across a calm section of water.

"You saved her, Jake. She loves being with you, being a part of your life."

"I can't take the place of her mother."

"No one can," Millie agreed. "But Stacy isn't here. You have to stop regretting what you can't change."

"Good advice." Jake picked up another rock. "Ever skipped stones?"

"Across the Potomac? Uh…no."

He took her hand and closed her palm around the rock, warmed from the sun and his touch. "It's all in the wrist action."

"Where have I heard that before?"

He laughed and shook his head. "Try it."

She concentrated and flipped the rock, watching as it sailed through the air and landed with a plop into the water.

He handed her another one, this time coming to stand behind her. His fingers covered hers, showing her the motion. With his body pressed to her back, Millie had trouble concentrating but eventually tossed the stone toward the creek. It hit the water then bounced twice before disappearing into the river.

"I did it." She spun around and grabbed his arms, bouncing on her toes. "I skipped it."

"You're a natural."

She sank back to her heels but didn't move away from him. His hands slid down her arms, making her tingle with need.

He leaned down, his mouth inches from hers. "You told me not to kiss you again."

"That was smart of me," she whispered then licked her suddenly dry lips.

His eyes smoldered. "Are you feeling smart right now, Millie?"

She felt many things right now, but the most prominent was a deep, aching desire to touch and be touched by Jake Travers. Definitely not smart, but she didn't care one bit.

Slowly, she wound her hands around his neck, closing the few inches between them. "I was never known for my brains," she said and closed her mouth over his.

Only to have him pull away. "Don't say that." He pressed a gentle kiss to her forehead. "You're smart, fierce and way more capable than you give yourself credit for, Millie Spencer."

She gasped a little, amazed at how much his words meant to her. How much she needed to hear them. She didn't know how to respond, nor did she trust her voice. Instead she kissed him again.

This time he didn't move from her. This time he kissed her as if his life depended on it, gently sucking her bottom lip into his mouth then running his tongue across the seam of her lips. She opened for him and the kiss turned deeper, hotter. Millie kept her eyes closed, reveling in the feel of him holding her close. His strong hands massaged the knots in her back as he drove her wild with his mouth.

She couldn't remember ever being so wrecked by a kiss. Despite what she knew was right, she wanted more. She'd told him they couldn't do this, but she needed him so badly.

He straightened suddenly just as she heard the sound of a horse whinnying nearby.

"We shouldn't—" she began.

"Don't, Millie. I'm not going to apologize and you won't tell me that was a mistake. Nothing that feels so damn good could be a mistake." He scrubbed his hand over his face. "This doesn't change anything. I want you. You want me. That doesn't mean I don't respect you. I'm not sure who did you wrong, but don't blame yourself or me for some other man's mistakes."

He was right. She knew it. Jake wasn't her father or any of the other men who had tried to take advantage of her. It wasn't his fault, but she couldn't quite let go of the belief that it might be hers.

"We should get back. I want to start dinner before Brooke gets home. She'll be wiped out after her first day of preschool and the afternoon out with her grandparents."

He looked at her intently, as if he wanted to say more. Finally he nodded and turned back toward the ranch.

I want you. That doesn't mean I don't respect you.

The words echoed in her head as they made their way along the path. He might respect her now, but how long would that last once he knew the whole truth?

Chapter Twelve

The next few weeks were the most normal that Jake could remember in his entire life. In fact, he was pretty sure he hadn't understood how much fun normal could be until he'd returned to Crimson.

With his leg unencumbered and his hand healing on schedule, he took the hospital's director, Vincent Gile, up on his suggestion that Jake help out in the free clinic at the hospital. Three times a week he volunteered during the morning hours—and sometimes late into the afternoon—seeing to indigent patients and those who needed but couldn't afford medical attention.

He'd been on the front lines of crisis medicine for so long, he'd forgotten how comforting it could be to simply help someone in need. It might not be as exciting or heart pumping as what he was used to, but the change suited Jake. Part of the reason he'd chosen to work with Miles of Medicine was because he didn't like staying in one place. The idea of establishing long-term relationships, especially with people who would depend on him, was bone-chillingly scary given how he'd failed his younger siblings for so many years.

Now it seemed like a challenge he was ready for, each patient a puzzle he looked forward to solving. Some of the cases were mundane but the gratitude he received from the clinic's patients made it well worth it. Crimson was a beautiful town, but not nearly as wealthy as nearby Aspen. Some people gave up a lot to live in the mountains. They worked hard but barely scraped by with the local cost of living. Jake was glad to help them and it was good to feel productive again. On the days he wasn't working, he spent the afternoons with Brooke and Millie or helping Logan on his kitchen renovation. He relished the normalcy of his own little slice of Americana in ways he hadn't believed possible.

His new appreciation of normal might explain why he was so pleased at the prospect of a couple of beers at the local bar after work. Or perhaps it was the woman fidgeting in the seat next to him. Jake pulled up to the curb and turned off the car.

"You didn't have to bring me with you," Millie said from her seat next to him.

"But I wanted to," he told her.

"I'm the nanny. What will your hospital friends think?" She tucked her hair behind her ear.

"That I've got more damn willpower than any guy imaginable to keep my hands off of you?"

Instead of making her laugh the way he'd intended, he saw the sides of her mouth pull down. "They'll think we're sleeping together," she muttered.

"Millie." He reached out and turned her face to his. "Why do you care what a bunch of people you don't know think about you?"

"Easy for you to say. You're 'the doctor,' the local hero come home. I'm nobody."

"Not to me." He sighed and rubbed his fingers along the back of her neck, trying to release some of the tension there. "We're friends. This is an engagement party for one of the nurses at the clinic. No one is going to be paying attention to you and me. Relax. This is supposed to be your night off. Our night off."

Logan and Olivia had invited Brooke for a sleepover, and to Jake's surprise, his daughter had wanted to go. Her grandparents had been shocked since Brooke had been adamant about not spending the night at their rented condo. She was okay when Janis and John took her for ice cream or to the park, but that was as much time as she'd spend with them. Jake didn't understand it but figured it had more to do with her wanting to stick close to him. But she hadn't hesitated when his brother came to pick her up tonight. She'd bounced down the steps toward Logan's truck, thrilled at the prospect of spending an evening baking with her Uncle Logan.

Jake hadn't planned to attend the hospital get-together, but he'd quickly realized that being in the house alone with Millie all night was going to be too much temptation. They hadn't kissed again since that day at Crimson Ranch, but he found himself wanting her more every moment.

Even now, when she was filled with unwarranted nerves. Everyone he knew loved Millie, from his family to the parents and kids at the preschool. She was a ray of sunshine everywhere she went, especially in his dull life.

"The people from the hospital are nice, Millie. And they're hardly my friends. I've worked with them a couple of weeks." He leaned closer. "You're my friend. We're going to have fun tonight. I promise."

Slowly, she nodded. “Sorry. I don’t know what’s wrong with me.”

“If you can tame a room full of rowdy preschoolers, hanging out with this bunch should be no problem.”

They walked together the half block to the bar, Jake resisting the urge to take her hand in his. He wasn’t lying when he told her she was his friend. Millie was probably the best friend he’d had in his life. He’d always lived alone, but now sharing the ups and downs of daily life with her, even in the short term, created a level of intimacy that went beyond his physical desire for her.

Sure, that was still there. Always there. At this point, wanting her seemed like the least of his worries. The way he depended on her as a part of his life was a lot scarier.

The bar, the Two Moon Saloon, was as crowded as he’d expect on a Friday night. It hadn’t changed much since Jake had come to retrieve his father here on weekend nights when he was a kid. Wood paneling still lined the walls and there was a mix of booths and four-top tables to one side of the room with a small dance floor near the back. In a far corner there were two pool tables and he noticed several people from the hospital gathered in that area. The beer signs that hung on the walls had been updated with labels of local and nationally known microbrews. But the bar still held the same somewhat sweet smell that he remembered—a strange combination of alcohol and perfume. The scent had made him want to retch as a kid.

As the oldest, Jake had been the one his mother sent to collect his dad on nights when he was too drunk to make it home on his own. Jake would make the twenty-minute trek from their ramshackle house into town and eventually coax his father to follow him home. He’d always tried not to make eye contact with any of the other customers or bartenders; he didn't want to know who was on hand to witness his dad's sloppy end to any given night.

Now he was surprised to find the smell didn't cause a reaction in him. Maybe it was because Millie was so close that the scent of her shampoo wafted up to him, covering the smells that evoked so much shame from his past.

One of the nurses waved them over to a couple of tables in front of the bar that had been pushed together. He made introductions and noticed that Millie's nervousness seemed to settle as she spoke with a few of the women. He recognized Natalie Holt and remembered that she was part of Millie's new group of friends.

He took a beer with his good hand when it was handed to him but didn't do more than sip on it. He'd never be much of a social drinker thanks to the memories he had of his father.

He sat with a couple of the other docs from the hospital. Lana Mayfield scooted a chair next to his after a few minutes.

"So what's your plan?" she asked when the people around them started in on a heated debate about the Broncos' prospects for the upcoming football season.

"Enjoy the evening," he answered, purposely misinterpreting her question. "Toast the happy couple."

She shook her head. "Come on, Jake. Your ankle is healed, and from everything I've seen, there won't be permanent nerve damage in your hand. I want to know what's next for you." She slid her hand along his shoulder, leaning so close that her breast pressed up against his arm. He could smell the hint of alcohol on her breath. "I'd like to be a part of your future."

He flexed his fingers around the bottle of beer on the table in front of him. As much as he'd wanted his hand to get better, he was ignoring the signs that pointed to a full recovery. As long as he could use his injuries as an excuse, he didn't need to deal with the decisions he'd have to make.

"It's complicated, Lana." He caught Millie looking at him from where she stood nearby with Natalie, but her gaze snapped away. "I've got to think of my daughter and what's best for her."

She wrinkled her nose. "I thought the grandparents were willing to take her."

"We'd agreed to that, yes. But things can change."

"You haven't changed, Jake. I don't believe it. You were the most single-minded person I'd ever met. You knew you wanted to be a doctor, how you wanted to practice medicine, and you made it happen. You're not the kind of person who settles down. You need the pressure and excitement to really feel alive." She pressed closer to him. "We both need that. We're two of a kind, you and me."

He doubted that. He moved his chair back, extricating himself from her awkward embrace.

"Anybody want to dance?" Natalie suddenly stood next to their table, Millie held at her side by Natalie's hand clamped around her wrist. "The DJ's just getting started." Her eyebrows rose as she glanced between Jake and Lana, disapproval clear on her pretty face.

Millie kept her head turned toward the dance floor.

"I wasn't much of a dancer before the accident," Jake admitted. "I think I'll pass."

"Are you sure?" Natalie tilted her head toward Millie. "Might be worth giving it a try."

"We're in the middle of a private conversation here," Lana told them, her eyes narrowed on Millie. "Discussing important hospital business. Doctor business. Neither of you would understand."

He was about to argue when Natalie leaned forward. "It doesn't take a medical degree to understand that you've got a stick lodged—"

"Come on, Nat." Millie tugged at her friend. "Let's go dance."

Damn. He ground his teeth as they walked away. He knew Millie had silly hang-ups about being in the company of people who were better educated than she, not that it mattered one bit to most people in Crimson. He didn't think Lana had been purposely cruel, but she was a snob. Jake couldn't believe he hadn't noticed what an irritating trait that was before now.

Maybe he wasn't a great dancer, but if it meant an excuse to get close to Millie, he was willing to give it a shot. She looked beautiful tonight, wearing a pale patterned blouse and a short denim skirt with sandals that laced around her ankles. Her skin glowed from the shimmery lotion that Brooke liked her to wear. He appreciated it for an entirely different reason and wanted the chance to touch Millie, to be close enough to have her scent invade his senses once again. He pushed back from the table before Lana's next comment stopped him.

"Looks like your nanny found a partner without you."

Millie and Natalie were dancing with a group of men—tourists, by the looks of their clothes. One of the guys—dark-haired, from what Jake could tell—took Millie's hand and twirled her as a popular country song rang out over the speakers. Jake took another drink of his beer and turned back to Lana, but his gaze kept straying to his lovely nanny on the dance floor.

After a few songs, Natalie, Millie and their entourage went to the bar for drinks. He saw the man lean into Millie and her laugh in response. She looked happy, fun and so full of life. This was where she was supposed to be, he realized, not stuck in the house with him and Brooke every night. This was the first time he'd seen her free-spirit side in action.

Soon the group around them had expanded. Jake realized that for all Millie's worry about fitting in, he was the one left on the outside. Too serious, too quiet. Just like he'd always been.

Lana never left his side, however, and after a while his head started to pound from her relentless hinting about their "possible future" together. Millie and the others had returned to the dance floor and he wasn't about to watch her enjoy herself in someone else's arms for a minute longer.

"I'm going to grab some air," he told Lana, standing.

"I'll go with you." Her smile was suggestive.

"That's okay. I'm not great company right now."

Before she could argue, he turned away. He wouldn't leave Millie here until he made sure Natalie would bring her home, but he needed to clear his head first. He hadn't seen how much Millie'd had to drink but was pretty certain the group had done at least a couple of shots.

He tried to keep his eyes focused on the exit, but his gaze slid to the dance floor once again. Through the crowd he caught sight of the dark-haired punk pulling Millie tight against his body. Jake was about to look away when he noticed the look of distaste on Millie's face. She shook her head and squirmed away but the guy held her tighter, bending to whisper something in her ear. She shook her head, the disapproval turning to fear in a split second.

Which was as long as it took Jake to change course, muscling his way through the other people on the dance floor. He pulled the man away by his shoulder, narrowly resisting the urge to punch the guy's smug face.

"What the—" the man sputtered as Jake put his arm around Millie, leading her away.

She looked up at him. Tears shimmered in her eyes. "You don't have to…"

"Let's go." Jake moved as quick as he could through the bar's customers toward the front door. He could tell Millie needed to get away.

The guy stepped in front of him, giving Jake a little shove. "Dude, she's with me. Find your own girl."

"Maybe you should take no for an answer, buddy. She's not with you anymore." Jake tucked Millie to his side, away from the man's grasp. "Get the hell out of my way."

"She wanted it." The man tilted his head toward Millie. "Some of them like it a little rough, you know."

A tremble rolled through Millie and he heard her give a little sob. That a jerk like this could bring her to tears infuriated Jake. And when the man reached for her, Jake's temper snapped. Without thinking he reached up and slammed his fist into the guy's face.

A searing pain sliced through Jake's arm. By instinct, he'd thrown the punch with his right hand. His injured hand. He sucked in a breath, trying not to let the pain take him down.

The man staggered back a few steps then steadied himself. He would have come at Jake, who was at a definite disadvantage with Millie plastered against him and the throbbing of his splinted hand.

But the bouncer from the front door wrapped his meaty arms around the guy. "Go on, Dr. Travers," he said to Jake. Jake recognized him from the clinic—he'd brought his mother in to be treated for a stomach infection last week. "I'll take care of this joker."

Jake made it out of the bar and a few steps down the sidewalk before he let go of Millie and doubled over in pain. He muttered every curse word in his vocabulary then gently flexed his fingers. At least they weren't broken.

"Oh, no." Millie was back at his side in an instant. "You hit him with your bad hand. What were you thinking?"

Jake straightened, taking deep gulps of the cool evening air. "I thought he was hurting you. That you were scared to pieces. I thought I was rescuing you."

"Who said I needed rescuing?" Her words were sharp but her tone gentle. She lifted his arm, cradling his hand in hers. She drew her fingers along his, raising them and kissing his knuckles that were already swelling. He felt a tear drop onto his finger and slip down the inside of his splint.

"Millie."

She shook her head, wiping the back of her sleeve across her face. "I'll drive home."

"You've been drinking."

"Fine." She kept her gaze averted from his but didn't let go of his hand. "You drive."

They walked to the car in silence, and the pain in his hand subsided to a dull ache.

He unlocked the car and opened the passenger-side door. Millie let go of his hand to climb into the Explorer.

"Millie, look at me. Please."

She turned, her emotions cut off from him.

"What happened back there?"

"You could have done permanent damage to your hand," she snapped. "It's not totally healed, Jake."

He shook his head. "On the dance floor. When that guy held on to you. Your reaction..."

"It was nothing. He freaked me out, that's all. I could have handled it." She bit down on her lip and Jake let it go because if there was one thing he didn't want, it was to make her cry again.

The ride home took only a few minutes. Millie looked out the window the entire time, her hands clasped tightly together in her lap. When he parked, she was out of the car like a shot, practically running up the front walk.

He trailed her into the house, expecting her to retreat to her bedroom, where she knew he wouldn't follow. Instead she went to the kitchen and, without flipping on a light, took one of Brooke's animal-shaped ice packs from the freezer. She returned to him, and he hissed as the cold touched his swollen skin.

"There was more to that than you being freaked out." He tipped up her chin. "You were scared, Millie. You should never be frightened of a man in that way."

He saw her swallow as she blinked several times. Damn. He hadn't wanted tears.

"It was my fault," she said after a moment, her voice just a whisper in the quiet house. "I led him on."

"You danced with him. I saw you. There was nothing more to it than that."

"I gave him ideas."

"Watching you floss your teeth would give a man ideas." That earned him a wisp of a smile. "It doesn't mean they get to act on them. You deserve to be cherished, Millie." He paused, unsure of how much to reveal. Then because the pain was clouding his mind, her scent was wreaking havoc on his senses and because the dark added some bit of protection, he added, "I would cherish you."

As she watched him, he saw in her eyes the same desire that coursed through him. But as much as he wanted to act on it, Jake held back. She was fragile at this moment, and he needed to be the kind of man who wouldn't take advantage of that.

So he began to move back, to leave her in peace as she'd once requested.

But when she rose up and brought her lips to his, all thoughts of leaving her alone vanished. He couldn't have pulled away from her at that moment if his life depended on it.

He let her choose. After what had happened to her at the bar, Jake didn't press her for more than she could give. He said he would cherish her and she believed him.

For that and so many other reasons, she wanted him.

She hadn't meant to lead the guy on in the bar. She'd only wanted to dance, get lost in the moment and try to drown out the disappointment she felt that Jake was spending his time with Lana. But Millie knew that sometimes men took more than she offered, felt as if they were entitled to more than she was willing to give.

Not Jake. It was virtually impossible for him to want more from her because she was ready to give him everything. That thought made emotion unfurl inside her chest. She pressed closer to him, wanting to lose herself in his strength, only to jump back with a gasp at the ice pack she held between them.

He took it from her hand and tossed it aside. She lifted her chilled fingers to the pulse beating in his throat.

He shuddered then bent to kiss the center of her palm. "Millie," he said in a husky tone, "I want you. All of you. But only if it's what you want, too."

"Yes." The syllable came out on a whoosh of air.

He lowered his mouth to hers, taking control of the kiss, deepening it then drawing back. He interlaced their fingers and led her through the darkened house down the hall to his bedroom.

Her eyes darted to Brooke's empty bedroom across the hall. Jake turned when she hesitated. "You can stop this at any time, Millie. Just walk away."

She didn't want the night to end, so she stepped forward, her hands splaying across his chest, and pushed him into his bedroom. His arms lowered to her waist and he lifted her as if she were no more than a child.

The feel of being in his arms, the safety and power of him, was all she'd imagined and more. Millie trusted him, perhaps not with her heart but definitely with her body.

He took the few steps to the bed and, stripping the quilt away, lowered her onto the sheets. Kneeling beside her, he undid first one sandal and then the next. He removed his splint then smoothed his palms up her bare legs to the backs of her knees, tickling the sensitive skin there.

She wiggled on the bed, unused to feeling so vulnerable in front of anyone. "I can handle this part."

"Let me," he said with a sexy smile, leaning forward to trail his mouth against her skin at the edge of her skirt.

Millie felt need and desire fan to life even brighter inside her. When he tugged the skirt down past her hips, she shut her eyes, unable to meet his gaze.

His fingers skirted the edge of her panties and she sent up a silent prayer of thanks that she'd at least put on decent underwear for the night. He began to work on the buttons of her shirt.

"Millie, open your eyes. Look at me." His voice was husky and low.

She took a breath and met his hot stare. "I'm not used

to this kind of attention," she whispered, trying to make a joke, but her voice caught on the last word.

"You should be. You should be cared for and worshipped. You are smart, clever and beautiful both inside and out." He spread the shirt open and she shivered as air touched the heated skin of her belly. "You deserve so much more than you've allowed yourself to have, Millie."

"Hey, Pot, meet Kettle," she answered without thinking. Then she could have kicked herself. Here was a man trying to make proper love to her, and thanks to her thrumming nerves, she was joking. Talk about looking a gift horse…

Jake threw back his head and laughed. "Come here," he told her and she rose to kiss him as he pushed the shirt off her arms. She could feel him smiling against her mouth but soon the kiss turned hot and needy again.

His fingers worked the clasp at the back of her bra and she clamped the front of it to her chest. Even though the lights were out, moonlight streamed in from the window. Millie felt suddenly exposed in a way she hadn't expected.

"Do you want to close the blinds?"

Jake nipped at the underside of her jaw. "Nope."

She gave him a little push. "Well, I'm not going to be the only one without my clothes on here."

He sat up and shucked his shirt over his head.

Heat radiated off his body, all sculpted lines and muscle. Two fading scars crisscrossed one shoulder, reminding her of what he'd been through. When she reached out to draw the tip of one finger down his chest, a tremble passed through him. Jake was holding himself back for her, and her heart opened to him because of it.

She moved forward, letting her bra drop as she molded her body to his. His touch turned possessive and hot and her body responded to him in the same way. His tongue traced the edge of her nipple before he took the peak into his mouth. Millie slid her fingers through his hair, urging him up to kiss her once more. They tangled together in the sheets, learning the nuances of each other. He continued to whisper sweet words to her, this Jake so different from the serious, sometimes emotionally distant man she'd first met.

He didn't leave any part of her unexplored, using his fingers then his mouth to bring her to the edge of desire. Millie wasn't totally inexperienced. She'd had a couple of boyfriends and understood sexual attraction. This was something totally different, so much more than she'd ever felt with a man.

Just as she thought she couldn't take any more of his teasing touch, he lifted away from her, taking a condom from the nightstand before he wrapped her in his arms again.

"Now?" he whispered and she marveled at his restraint.

Unable to speak, she nodded and opened to him completely.

She loved the feel of him around her and then inside her. Pressure built and she scraped her fingernails along the hard planes of his back, drawing a hoarse moan from him in response. As much as she wanted to hold back a part of herself, Millie didn't do things in half measures. When she gave herself over to him and to her own pleasure, she knew the highest peak of bliss and also the nagging sense she had lost herself to this man and it would likely end in heartbreak.

But that was a worry for another night.

Jake kept her cradled in his arms as she drifted to sleep then woke her hours later with soft, warm kisses along her spine. They made love again, lazily, taking their time with each other and the passion that banked between them.

When morning came, the dawning light had her questioning her sanity. She cursed her lack of willpower and the fact that she'd let her heart lead her down a path her head knew would be her downfall. She needed to collect herself, to gain some physical and emotional distance. She was an expert at compartmentalizing. If only she could figure out where to put last night, Millie thought she might have a chance at making it through the next several weeks.

She went to climb from the bed, but Jake pulled her back against him.

"Are we okay, Millie?"

"We're great, although we're going to be late for breakfast if I don't get in the shower." They were meeting Olivia, Logan and Brooke at Life Is Sweet later that morning.

"This doesn't have to change anything."

It changes everything.

"I know." She squirmed out of his embrace, feeling emotion knot in her chest. She didn't want to talk now, didn't trust herself to speak without revealing her feelings for him. She knew from her mother that showing her heart would give him the upper hand. If she kept her heart guarded, she could hold on to her power. She'd watched her mother give away her power over and over again, watched it seep out of her, leaving her a shell of a woman whose only purpose in life was to keep a man happy.

Millie couldn't let herself fall into the same trap. She was overreacting, but she couldn't help it. This was the exact reason she'd limited herself to only casual relationships. She was wired just like her mother, and it had always terrified her that with one misstep, she'd find herself down the same rabbit hole.

Taking the sheet with her, she grabbed her clothes from the floor and retreated to the other end of the house. She turned the water in the shower as hot as she could stand it, hoping the heat would burn away her fears and regret. One night, she admonished herself. It didn't have to mean anything. Jake had told her as much.

The shower door slid back, and she started as Jake climbed in with her, filling up the small space. She stepped away, her back practically pressed to the cold tile, and wrapped her arms around herself.

"What are you doing?"

He reached out, but instead of touching her, he adjusted the nozzle above his head so that water once again sprayed down on her, keeping her warm. As if his proximity wasn't enough.

"Does last night change things, Millie?"

She wiped at her face, blinking to see him clearly. "You said yourself it doesn't." She jerked her thumb toward the bathroom. "There isn't exactly room enough for two in here."

One side of his mouth curved. "There's plenty of room." He snagged her hand and placed it on his bare chest, over his heart. She focused on the steady beat of it as he spoke.

"I said it doesn't *have* to change anything. Not that I don't want it to." His heartbeat increased its pace. "This is new to me, Millie. Everything about this past month has been new to me. I don't know what the hell I'm doing, and I don't want to hurt you in the process. You get to decide. If this is more than one night, I'll be thrilled. If last night was an aberration, I'll respect that. You choose."

Once again, he was giving her the power. He meant it, she knew, but in putting the decision in her hands he was cracking the last of her defenses. She wanted so much more from this man than he probably knew how to give. She took a breath, ready to tell him that they couldn't go forward.

The look of vulnerability in his eyes stopped her. His heart beat like crazy beneath her fingers and she knew she wasn't alone in her fear. Their pasts and the emotional scars they'd both buried so deep bonded them. It was a link, maybe even a foundation. For the first time Millie thought she might have a chance of being on equal footing in a relationship. These were uncharted waters for both of them. Maybe together was the only way to make it through to calmer seas.

"I choose you," she said softly. "I choose us."

His eyes closed for a moment and she saw him take a shuddering breath. But when he opened them again, the vulnerability was gone, replaced by smoldering desire.

"Then let's see if we can't make this shower fit the both of us," he said and drew her to him once again.

Chapter Thirteen

Jake found himself distracted for the next several days as Millie's words echoed in his head.

I choose us.

When had he ever been anyone's choice? He'd always worked and fought for what he wanted, and all he'd ever focused on was work. Now he had so many other things to occupy his time.

His cell phone beeped again, another text coming through. Another text that he ignored. He'd been avoiding the director of the agency for the past week. A few of his coworkers had called, too. There was never any lack of projects and needs, and Jake had always been the doctor most willing to travel on a moment's notice to far-flung locations with minimal facilities. Substandard accommodations and difficult cases had been part of the appeal to him, a way to challenge himself while remaining emotionally uninvolved.

Now he couldn't believe he'd ever been satisfied living like that. His time with Millie and Brooke had made him long for more, allowed him to believe a normal family life might be attainable for someone like him.

He still got daily reminders that he was in over his head. Today's came at rehearsal for Brooke's preschool fall musical. The program was some sort of mountain-animal festival. Each of the kids was supposed to be a tree, flower or critter from around the area. It was hard for Jake to tell them apart. He saw a couple of kids with brown felt draped over their shoulders and small headbands that had ears sticking out. Bears, he assumed.

"Aren't the costumes perfect?"

Jake turned to see one of the mothers standing next to him.

"Um…sure. Very creative."

She smiled. "I made most of them myself."

He'd gotten to know a few of the parents, but because Millie worked at the school he'd left most of the mommy socializing to her.

"Your nanny does a great job with the kids."

He nodded as Millie wiped the tears of a crying girl. Laura Wilkes had put Millie in charge of today's rehearsal. Brooke waved to him from where she stood near the far side of the makeshift stage. They'd cleared out the preschool room to use for the program. He waved to his daughter, who was dressed as a…

"She makes a very cute fox."

A fox. Right. That was what he was going to guess.

Millie came over to them. The girl who had been crying was holding her hands together in front of her costume's lower half.

"It's hard to remember to take a potty break when there's so much excitement," Millie said. "Can one of you help the kids run through the rest of the program while I help her change clothes?" She handed a notebook to Jake. "Here are the notes for the performance."

Before he could answer, she walked away toward the bathroom. He looked to the other mom, holding out the notebook.

"Sorry." She shook her head. "I just stopped by to drop off my son's snack. I have to pick up his older sister at dance class." She patted Jake on the shoulder. "You'll be fine."

Just like that, Jake was left on his own with over a dozen preschoolers looking at him. His heart pounded as he took a step toward them. One of the boys stuck his finger up his nose and another girl's lip trembled.

"Daddy, why do you look so angry?" Brooke pulled on the front of her fox costume, which consisted of a red sweater and pointy ears. "You're scaring Helena. And Derek is eating his boogers, which is disgusting. And someone didn't flush today when they went number two. And—"

Jake held up a hand. "Okay, Cookie. Thanks for sharing all of that."

He pointed at the girl with the quivering lip. "You. Helena, right? No tears, got it?"

Helena nodded even as tears streaked down her cheeks.

"No tears!"

"Daddy, stop yelling." Brooke walked over to Helena. "Come and stand next to me. I'll protect you."

"Protect her from me?" Jake eyed his daughter. Panic bubbled up in him. Were fathers supposed to know how to deal with groups of kids? Wasn't that what moms were for? His daughter was stuck with him. While he was clueless.

She threw him a look. "Daddy, take care of the boogers."

He tried. Really, he tried. But it was as if the kid hadn't eaten in weeks and snot was on the dessert buffet.

Fifteen minutes later, Jake was drenched in sweat and his head pounded. The kids had abandoned pageant rehearsal and were running circles around him. Literally.

He tried grabbing for one of the boys, but the kid ducked away from his grasp. Then all of the children stilled. Jake turned around to the sound of singing. Millie walked back into the room, singing a song about children stopping their play so they could listen to her.

And they did.

Jake had tried yelling, pleading, bribes, whatever he could think of, but nothing had worked. All Millie did was sing a little ditty and they fell into line like a platoon of army cadets.

Amazing.

She was amazing.

"How's it going?"

"Perfect," he answered, wiping his brow.

She flashed a knowing smile. "Not always as easy as it looks."

"It never looked easy," he muttered.

She rounded up the kids then directed Jake to help them take off their costumes and hang them for safekeeping.

Parents, mostly mothers, began trickling in to pick up their children. They seemed impressed that Jake was there helping. He felt like a total fraud as they discussed plans for the pageant, volunteer roles, snack charts and other things most mothers seemed to know intrinsically. He smiled and nodded, but was secretly relieved when he was left alone with Brooke and Millie.

Jake sank into one of the tiny chairs at the preschool

table, his knees practically level with his chin. Millie bustled around the room, humming under her breath as Brooke scooped dried beans from a small plastic pool in the center of the room then spilled them out again. Dried beans as a toy—one more thing he would have never thought of.

After a moment, Millie came up behind him. Her legs pressed against his back as she bent to swiftly kiss his cheek while Brooke was occupied. They'd agreed to keep their relationship quiet since it was so new. He imagined his daughter would love the thought of Millie as a potential stepmother, but Jake wasn't ready to go down that road quite yet.

"That was awful," he said with a groan.

Millie ran her fingers through his hair. "You managed."

"Hardly. I made a girl cry and watched one of the boys attempt to eat his weight in snot."

"Derek," Millie answered without hesitation. "We're working on that."

"I totally panicked, Millie. Those kids looked to me. I was in charge. I couldn't handle it." He shook his head. "Janis would have known what to do."

"Jake..." Millie's tone was patient. "You're a dad, not a child-care expert. You did fine. The kids survived."

"No thanks to me."

"Why are you being so hard on yourself?" She lowered herself to the chair next to him, patting his arm, her gaze sympathetic. "You've got years to get good at this."

He suppressed a shudder. "That's just it. What if I never get good? What if I don't want to?" He felt her gaze on him but couldn't look at her. "I'm a doctor. I know how to sew up the human body, but the thought of making a costume for my daughter is terrifying."

"You buy them online," she countered.

"That's not the point and you know it. I want to be a part of Brooke's life. I love her and can't imagine life without her. But I still don't believe I'm her best bet for every day."

"You're her father."

"That's biology. Lord knows my father didn't add a damn thing except misery to my childhood. Yours wasn't much different. I might do more harm than good to her. That would kill me."

"You won't, Jake."

"You don't know that." He shook his head as he watched his daughter. "Janis and John are pressuring me about a custody agreement. The agency is pressuring me to commit to a timeline for returning to the field."

Millie stiffened. It was the first time he'd mentioned going back to his old job. "I thought you liked working at the hospital here."

"I do, but it's temporary."

"It doesn't have to be."

"I'm not cut out for this," he whispered. "As much as you want it to be."

"Me?" She stood. "This isn't about me. It's about the daughter who needs you in her life."

"I'd be in her life. Only not the way *you* want me to." He turned away, unwilling to see the disappointment he knew he'd find in her gaze. It was the same emotion he'd read on the faces of his brothers and sister when he left home, and he couldn't stand to fail someone he cared about again.

Millie heard the door to the preschool open as Jake's words trailed off. He was right to stop this argument, of course, for many reasons. But she didn't want it to end without convincing him that she was right. She couldn't let go of her determination to see him settled as a full-time father for Brooke.

But when she caught sight of the woman peeking her head around the door to the main room, Millie's heart took off at a frantic pace.

She whirled as Jake stood up behind her, his finger resting lightly on her back as if to give her support. She stepped away from his touch.

"Mrs. Bradley," she said, taking a hesitant step forward. "What are you doing in Crimson?"

"Hello, Millie." The woman adjusted her bun and gave the room an approving glance. "You didn't return my calls, so I contacted your sister. She told me I could find you here."

Millie's heart sank as she thought about how much detail Karen Bradley might have shared with Olivia. Jake cleared his throat behind her.

"Oh, right," Millie sputtered. "This is…" She paused, as if she'd forgotten Jake's name. "Let me introduce you to—"

"I'm Jake Travers," he said, reaching out a hand.

"Karen Bradley, dean of the College of Education from the University of Las Clara."

"Mrs. Bradley was my course adviser when I was at school," Millie told him.

Jake nodded. "Millie works for me here in Crimson."

"Works for you?" Karen's brows furrowed. "I thought you worked at the preschool, Millie."

Before Millie could answer, Brooke ran forward. "Millie is a Fairy Poppins. That means she's my nanny." The little girl pushed her hair back from her face. "I'm Brooke. He's my daddy." She pointed to Jake. "My mommy died when she went to find him. She's in heaven now, but I wish she was still here with me."

Karen's gaze didn't waver from Brooke's. Karen Bradley was an expert on early childhood education, having spent her career teaching and writing books that were used in college classrooms around the country. Millie had always felt intimidated by her faculty adviser, but she trusted that Karen could handle Brooke's honesty about her mother's death. "That must have been very hard for you." She bent to Brooke's level as she spoke.

The girl nodded in response. Her fingers flexed as if she was holding Bunny to her side, but the stuffed animal was tucked away in one of the preschool cubbies. It had been a big step for Brooke to relinquish her hold on Bunny during preschool hours and now Millie wanted the girl to have the comfort of the familiar lovey in her arms.

"It's good that your daddy is here for you."

"When I had my birthday party, I wished for a daddy. I told Mommy I would trade all my presents for having a daddy like my friends. He was my birthday wish, so Mommy went to get him for me." She spread her arms wide. "But there was a big earf-quake and she got dead."

Millie heard Jake suck in a breath and realized she was holding hers. None of them had understood exactly what had prompted Stacy Smith to seek out Jake when he'd known nothing about Brooke for years. She realized it was the girl's own request. Somehow it made Jake's presence in Brooke's life all the more poignant.

"You're a brave girl, Brooke."

Brooke looked to Millie. "Can I get Bunny out of his cubby?"

"Of course."

As the girl left the room, Millie dabbed at the corner of her eye. She couldn't make eye contact with Mrs. Bradley or Jake.

"I'm sorry for your loss," she heard Karen say to Jake.

"It's not… We weren't… It's a long story." He touched Millie's elbow. "Do you two need some privacy?"

"That would be—" Karen began at the same time Millie said, "Nope. All good here."

She dug deep and managed to produce a sunny smile. "Mrs. Bradley, are you on vacation?" She gave a laugh that sounded forced even to her own ears. "I'm happy you looked me up but I don't know—"

"It's about Daniel Blaine." Karen's eyes flicked to Jake. "Are you sure you don't want to speak about this alone?"

Millie was certain she didn't want to speak about Daniel Blaine at all. "I don't know what there's left to say. Two sides of the story and all that. I learned an important lesson so—"

"Two other women have come forward and made accusations about his inappropriate advances."

"Oh."

"Inappropriate advances," Jake repeated. "What is that about?" He turned to Millie. "Did some man hurt you, Millie?"

"No." She shook her head. "It wasn't like that. I didn't think…" She glanced at Karen Bradley. The woman studied her with a mix of understanding and sympathy. "I think Mrs. Bradley and I do need a few minutes. Jake, I'll lock up here and meet you back at the house." She kept her gaze trained on the floor.

"Are you sure? I can stay or call Olivia if you need support." He reached out for her but she shrugged away.

"I'm on her side," she heard Karen say.

She watched Jake begin to walk away but didn't hear his response through the roaring in her ears. After a few moments, she sank down into the child-sized chair once more. "Why did you come here to tell me this?"

Karen remained standing. "Several reasons. You were

put on academic probation because of the incident between you and Daniel."

"Because no one believed me," Millie said on a hiss of breath. Anger and humiliation washed over her as she thought of that time.

"I'm sorry." Karen lowered herself to the edge of the table. "I'm here to apologize and make things right with you." She paused then added, "We also need you to come back and make a formal statement. Testify, if necessary."

Millie lifted her head. "Come back?"

Karen nodded. "We need you, Millie."

It was close to seven before Millie returned to Jake's house. After her conversation with Karen, she'd walked the streets of Crimson. In her short time here, she'd come to love this tiny town. She passed the older section, with houses in neat rows, and imagined settlers who had founded Crimson making their way over the mountains to begin a new life. They were people of great strength who had tamed these wild lands. She knew some had come for the chance of striking gold and making their fortune, but others came for a fresh start.

She understood why. The mountains could be grounding, inspiring and humbling all at the same time. She could imagine a place in this community, but her conversation with Karen Bradley had been a reminder that Crimson wasn't her home.

It had been so easy to leave the past behind, to ignore it in place of pretending that she was a clean slate. But that wasn't the case, and she couldn't move forward without dealing with everything that had come before.

Jake was just reading Brooke a story when Millie got to the house.

“Do you have time for a good-night song, Brookie-Cookie?” Millie asked from the girl’s bedroom door.

“Millie!” Brooke held open her arms, and Millie came forward to give her a hug, breathing in the smell of her watermelon shampoo and clean soapy skin.

She loved this little girl, just as she loved Brooke’s father.

The realization, while not new, came as a shock just the same. She couldn’t make eye contact with Jake, who rose from the bed when she sat down.

“Night, sweetie,” he said, bending forward to ruffle Brooke’s hair. He placed a soft kiss on top of the girl’s head. Millie remembered that first day at the house when Jake had seemed almost afraid to touch his daughter. He’d come so far. She wanted to beg him not to give up now.

With Brooke tucked into bed, Millie made her way back to the center of the house. Jake sat on the couch, the end-table light the only thing illuminating the large family room.

“Thanks for taking care of things,” she said. “I didn’t mean to leave you on your own for the whole night.”

He pierced her with his gaze. “Come here, Millie.”

“I’m pretty tired. Long day, you know.”

“I know we need to talk about what that woman said to you.”

Millie paused and tried to look casual. “It’s fine. Misunderstanding. We got it all worked out.”

“Does Olivia know?”

“Nothing happened,” Millie answered, unable to keep the edge out of her voice.

“If you don’t come and explain it to me, I’m going to call your sister.”

“Is that a threat?”

"I don't care what you call it. I want to know what happened to you."

Millie knew he wasn't going to give up. As much as she didn't want to talk about this, it would be easier with Jake than Olivia. Her sister had a protective streak a mile long and Millie figured she'd never hear the end of it if Olivia got involved.

She sat gingerly on the edge of the couch, not trusting herself to be too close to Jake.

"I promise it's not a big deal. There was a little trouble with the principal at the elementary school where I interned. It's fine now."

"Did he hurt you?" Jake's voice was soft but laced with ice.

"No." She took a breath. "Not really. He was so helpful and supportive when I started. We were friends and he was like a mentor to me. We got close, but he misinterpreted how close I wanted to be."

"What did he do?"

She flicked her fingers. "He got a little handsy, you know."

"I don't know. Explain it."

Millie felt as if she was being interrogated and crossed her arms over her chest, not liking what the situation revealed about her and her weakness. "He tried to kiss me, made it clear that he wanted our relationship—if that's what you could call it—to go to the next level."

"A level that involved sex?"

Jake's bluntness made her wince. "He said that my reference letter was tied to how I performed in all aspects of the job."

"Sexual harassment."

"We'd gone out for drinks. I liked him—not like that but I thought I could trust him. He was married, with kids, and had a great reputation at the college. His school staff loved him. He said I'd given him mixed signals and I couldn't be trusted with dads. That I'd be a dangerous teacher because I made men want me. He told me no one would trust me with their children." Saying the words out loud made the humiliation burn hot and bright in her throat once again.

"You know that's crap, right?"

"I do now. But..." Her voice trailed off.

"But what?"

She made herself look him in the eye, despite her embarrassment. "But that's how my mom managed her life. Not that she wasn't faithful to my father. She was. But whether it was him or the mechanic or the landlord, she would bat her eyes and smooth talk the men in her life into helping her and taking care of whatever needed fixing. It was an art form for her and one of the few things she tried to teach me when I was growing up."

She took a breath. "She told me it's where my power came from, but I watched her give hers away every time she made herself into nothing more than an object for those men. I vowed never to live my life that way. Sometimes I think I have too much of her in me, that I can't help myself."

Shifting on the sofa, she ran her fingers along a seam on one of the cushions. "That's what Daniel Blaine told the people at the university. I was so embarrassed I didn't mention it to anyone. But he was afraid I would, so he beat me to it. He went to the academic board and my adviser—Karen Bradley—and said that I'd come on to him. Of course I denied it but the damage was already done."

"They believed him?"

"Most of them did. Karen had doubts, but there wasn't anything she could do."

"She could have stood up for you."

Millie shrugged. "She did her best. I was close to being expelled. She made sure I only got academic probation for a semester." Millie hated that her eyes filled with tears. "I'd put all of my money into school and it left me at loose ends. So I came here. Olivia had been so nice when we met, but she doesn't owe me anything. I don't want her involved in cleaning up my mess."

"She loves you, Millie. She's your sister."

"My mom loves me, too. That didn't mean she had my best interest at heart. I love being in Crimson. But Karen wants me to go back to California. Daniel accosted two other student teachers. It went pretty far with one of them." She shook her head. "If only they'd believed me, maybe this wouldn't have happened. If I was more reliable, if I looked like someone who wouldn't get into that kind of trouble." She gave a watery laugh. "Heck, if I looked like Olivia, the situation would have ended a different way."

"It isn't your fault." Jake stood then moved to sit next to her. He took her hands in his. She felt her fingers shaking, but somehow didn't mind Jake seeing her so vulnerable. "You can't blame yourself because some guy took advantage of you."

"If I hadn't—"

"Enough. You didn't do anything wrong."

She couldn't remember ever wanting to lean on someone the way she did Jake. It felt totally right when he pulled her into his lap. His hand came around her neck, slowly massaging the muscles there. With a sigh, she let her cheek drop to his shoulder. They stayed that way for several minutes, Jake's strong presence relaxing her.

"What happens next?" he asked quietly.

She thought about that for a while before speaking. “I go back.”

“When?” She felt him tense beneath her. “For how long?”

“I won’t leave you and Brooke in a lurch. Karen wants me to fly to California next week to make a formal statement. It will only take a day. I’ve already called Olivia and she can help out with Brooke while I’m away. I made a commitment and I’ll honor that.”

“That’s not what I mean.”

“I ran away, Jake.” She burrowed into his shoulder. “I should have fought harder to have them believe me. I should have fought Daniel more. I want to be a teacher. I think I’d be good at it.”

“You’ll be an amazing teacher, Millie. Anyone can see that.”

“Just like you’re turning into a great father.”

He gave a small laugh. “Nice change of topic. But this time it’s about you.”

“It’s about us both.” She drew in another breath and met his gaze. “We’re in limbo together.”

“It’s a limbo, then?”

“You know what I mean. Each of us is trying to figure out what’s next. You with Brooke, and me with another chance to finish my education.”

“In California,” he supplied.

“For a time, yes.”

He didn’t respond to that, only continued to look at her with a gaze that warmed her to her toes. She was wrapped in Jake’s embrace, the silence of the house creating what felt like a cocoon for the two of them. At this moment, she didn’t want to think about the future or what would happen—or not—between them. She only wanted to be here, now, with him.

She leaned forward and touched her tongue to the seam of his lips.

"Millie," he whispered. "You don't have to do this. You've been through a lot today."

"I want this." She nipped at the corner of his mouth. "I want you."

He slanted his mouth over hers, deepening the kiss. It told her that he felt the same and even more. Without words, he told her everything she needed to know.

His hands moved on her skin, and desire built in her.

"I want you in my bed. Beneath me, on top of me, any way you'll have me."

She knew those were only love words. He couldn't really mean them because what she wanted was his whole heart. She didn't believe Jake was ready for that.

She untangled from his embrace and stood. Disappointment flashed across his face until she reached out her hand to him. "Stay with me."

The request almost felt silly since they'd lived under the same roof for nearly a month now, but he laced his fingers with hers as if he might understand her unspoken desire. He followed her to her bedroom and they undressed each other slowly, discovering the intricacies of each other's bodies as they whispered words of need and want.

When they lay wrapped together a long time later, Millie felt Jake begin to drift to sleep then tense. "I should go back to my room," he said, kissing the tip of her nose.

"In the morning," she whispered, snuggling deeper into him.

When he remained rigid, she clasped her hands on either side of his head. "You can trust yourself with me."

His features gentled and he kissed her again. "How do you always know what I'm thinking?"

"I know you."

"The nightmares come when I'm deep in sleep, Millie. If I'm here with you and I strike out, I could hurt you."

"You won't hurt me, Jake." She traced the skin under his eyes. "When was the last time you had a decent night's sleep? I've seen your phone. You set the alarm to go off every hour in the night. That isn't restful."

He shrugged. "If I wake myself up at regular intervals, the dreams don't seem to come. That's what I always do, but I'm not sure I can manage it in your room. It's worth it not to disturb Brooke. I don't want her to be scared of me. I remember what that was like."

"Your father was a horrible man. That's not who you are."

He eased away from her. "It's still better this way."

"No." She drew him back against her. "Try it tonight, Jake. I'm a light sleeper. If you get agitated, I'll move away."

"You're so precious, Millie." He stared at her, as if trying to solve a puzzle, then took a short breath and relaxed onto his back, moving her so she lay sprawled across his chest. "You go to sleep. I'll stay here until you are."

She knew this was an argument she wouldn't win, so she agreed. But several minutes later, she felt his breathing turn regular and she knew he'd succumbed to exhaustion. Millie lay there several more minutes, savoring his warmth around her. Soon her own eyes drifted shut, and she didn't fight that, either.

Chapter Fourteen

Jake woke in the early morning more rested than he'd felt in months. He hadn't left Millie's bed, but no bad dreams had plagued him. He'd held her tight against him, his own personal security blanket. As she'd promised, her warm presence had kept the nightmares at bay.

He leaned forward to kiss her neck. She sighed and smiled, turning until she was facing him. Her eyes didn't open but she brought her arms around him, drawing him in for a passionate kiss then deep inside her, their lovemaking slow and sweet.

When he finally left her bed, he put more ice on his hand, then walked quietly back to his side of the house before Brooke woke. He felt normal, which was something new for him. It was something he could get used to.

He'd taken on an extra shift at the clinic today, so when Brooke wasn't looking he gave Millie a quick kiss then said goodbye to his daughter.

"Why do you have to leave, Daddy?" Brooke asked, turning those big blue eyes on him.

"I'm only going to work, Brookie-Cookie. I'll be back before you know it."

"You work too much," she complained. "Mommy did, too, and then she died."

"I'm not going to die," he answered after a startled moment. "You've been to the hospital. You know it's safe there."

Brooke stomped her foot. "I don't want you to go. What if you don't come back?"

He glanced to Millie for some relief, but she gave him a small shake of her head. He was on his own. Great.

He bent lower to look into his daughter's eyes. "Nothing is going to happen to me, Brooke."

"What if it does?"

"It won't."

"But what if—"

"Enough." He stood and drew in a breath. His daughter's sweet chin trembled as she watched him. He'd raised his voice, and suddenly he was transported back to his own childhood, to being afraid to ever speak, never knowing what kind of response he was going to get from his father, whose mercurial moods could change in an instant.

"I promise I'll be back," he said, gentling his tone. He wasn't used to having his schedule questioned. Normally he could go wherever he wanted whenever he wanted. No one bothered to care. Things were different now, he knew, but it was an adjustment. "You have preschool. I have work. It will be okay." He felt out of his element but he bent and picked up his daughter. "I love you, Brooke." He realized it was the first time he'd said the words out loud.

She gave him a small smile. "Love you, too, Daddy."

He breathed in her sweet scent, layered with a little bit of syrup after this morning's pancake breakfast.

Dropping from his embrace, she started toward her bedroom. "I'm going to get dressed. Millie, will you make my hair in braids?"

"Sure thing." As Millie walked past him, she brushed another kiss on his cheek. "You're a good man, Jake Travers."

Her belief in him made Jake feel as if he'd just won the lottery. When he got to the hospital, Vincent called him into his office and made a formal offer of employment. Jake had guessed it was coming and hadn't known how he'd feel about truly settling down. Then he remembered the way his daughter's eyes had lit up when he'd told her he loved her and how much she wanted him as a part of her life.

Didn't he owe it to her and to himself to really make that commitment?

His mind formed a picture of Brooke, Millie and him as a family, with a little brother or sister added to the mix. His heart began to race, but not in panic. What he felt was anticipation in a way he hadn't looked forward to the future in a long time.

Unfortunately, his mood didn't last. There had been an explosion at one of the silver mines north of town and half a dozen men were brought in with a variety of injuries. The intensity of the work tested his stamina and his focus. He lost himself in the familiar exhilaration of crisis medicine, so absorbed in what he was doing that he didn't give a thought to the clock.

This was his skill set, his training and where he was most comfortable. He kept working until all of the patients were stable and either discharged or admitted. Adrenaline kept him moving when his leg started to throb and his wrist ached. But his hand held up through the entire day, with none of the nerve pain he'd become accustomed to feeling.

At some point, he'd misplaced his cell phone, so he'd given the reception desk Millie's number and asked them to call and relay a message that he'd be home later than expected.

By the time he pulled onto his street, fatigue was starting to set in. That changed when he saw the fire truck in front of the house. He parked and ran through the front door.

Brooke was the first to spot him. "Daddy, you didn't come back," she yelled. "You left and we needed you and you didn't come home."

"I'm sorry, Cookie," he said, his hammering heart starting to slow at the realization that his daughter wasn't hurt.

He ignored Janis's disapproving stare and swung Brooke into his arms, hugging her tight. "I'm here now. What's going on?"

"Fairy Poppins got dead for a few minutes. I was bleeding and it killed her."

His heart took off once again.

"I'm okay," Millie called from the couch. Two large EMT workers blocked her from view. "Not a big deal. Sorry for all the trouble."

He put Brooke down and strode forward, elbowing one of the guys out of the way. The other had his hands in Millie's hair and frowned. "Excuse me, sir. We're working here."

"I'm a doctor." Jake nudged the man aside. Both EMTs were young and stepped back in deference to Jake. "Tell me what happened."

He'd been talking to Millie, but the taller EMT recited

her injuries. "She has head trauma, a skin laceration. It doesn't look like a concussion, but that's a possibility."

"I don't have a concussion," she said, her eyes rolling.

He held up a hand, silencing the EMT. "Talk to me," he said as he spread her hair to examine the cut on the back of her head.

"Brooke cut herself. I'm not great with blood. I fainted, but luckily the edge of the counter broke my fall." She flashed a wan smile that he didn't return. "That led to more blood and I passed out again." She must have read the look on his face because she quickly added, "It was only a few minutes."

"Thank heavens we stopped by when we did." Janis had come to stand behind him, holding Brooke's hand. "This poor thing was scared to death."

Jake turned, noticing Brooke held Bunny in a death grip once again.

"You were 'posed to come back, Daddy."

"I'm sorry," Millie whispered.

At that moment, Olivia hurried into the house.

"What the hell," Jake muttered.

"Sorry," Millie said again. "I called my sister when Brooke's grandparents showed up. You weren't answering your phone. I wanted…someone here for me."

His gaze crashed into hers and he thought he read the words she'd left unspoken clearly in her eyes. *Because you weren't.*

Olivia came forward and Brooke ran to her. "Aunt Livvy, Millie almost got dead like Mommy."

"Oh, sweetie." Olivia hugged her. "Millie is just fine."

Brooke gave a small nod. "I got a cut, too." She tipped her chin to show off the bandage there. "I bleeded a whole lot."

"It's a good thing you're so brave." Jake watched as Olivia met Millie's eyes. "You okay?"

"I'll be better as soon as people stop hovering over me." Millie's voice sounded thin and embarrassed, as if she'd done something wrong.

Jake didn't understand, but he hustled the two EMTs out of the house. From what he could tell, Millie didn't need stitches and he planned to keep a very close eye on her in case she had any post-concussive symptoms.

When he came back, Millie was sitting up on the couch, Brooke tucked in at her side.

He saw Janis down the hallway, carrying his daughter's small backpack, and walked over to meet her before she was within earshot. "I'm going to take Brooke home with me." She glared at Jake, as if daring him to argue.

Which he was happy to do given his mood. "How is that going to help?"

"You didn't see the look on her face, Jake. She was terrified. After everything that girl has been through, she needs stability. She needs to be taken care of by people who will put her needs first."

"I'm here, Janis. I'm in Crimson with Brooke doing my best to make this work."

She gave a hard shake of her head. "Not good enough. My daughter died trying to give Brooke a father. Stacy put everything in her life on hold. She dedicated herself to Brooke. She did it alone."

"Because she never, in four years, thought to mention to me that I had a daughter. That isn't my fault."

"No," the woman agreed after a moment. "But you hired a nanny." The fact that she put air quotes around the word *nanny* grated on Jake's nerves. "A nanny who passes out at the sight of blood. One you can't take your eyes from most of the time." Her gaze narrowed. "Don't think I haven't noticed. The two of you playing at whatever games you like. What kind of a role model are you for my granddaughter? That's not how Stacy would have wanted her raised. She would have wanted her daughter to be brought up in a stable, steady home." She took a breath and her tone softened. "I know that's not what you had as a boy, Jake. I've asked around town about your family."

"You had no right—"

"When it comes to protecting my granddaughter, I don't give a horse's patoot about minding my own business. That girl is my business. I believe you want what's best for her. John and I can give her a stable home. Tonight proves she belongs with us."

What tonight proved was that Jake's life was more damned complicated than he'd even imagined.

"Please, let me take her." Janis's voice broke and he saw tears swim in her eyes.

He blew out a breath. "She can spend the night with you. That's as much as I can promise for now." But he knew he'd give more. He'd let Janis and John raise his daughter because it would be best for Brooke. As much as he tried, Jake didn't believe he would ever deserve to be her full-time father. She was worth so much more than he could give her.

Emotion tightened his throat. He turned before Janis could see his heart breaking. "Cookie," he said, coming to the couch but not meeting Millie's intense gaze, "you're going to spend the night with Nana and Papa. How does that sound?"

Brooke shook her head. "I want to stay here. So you don't leave and Millie doesn't die."

"I'm going to be just fine, sweetie." Millie hugged her

hard. "Remember I'm taking my trip to California tomorrow. I'll be back to tuck you in at bedtime, though."

"Daddy needs me," Brooke said, her innocent gaze trained on Millie.

Millie smiled gently. "Of course he does. You'll always be there for him. Just like he will for you."

The words gnawed at Jake's insides as if Millie had chosen them for that very purpose.

She sat up straighter, lifting Brooke onto her lap. "But tonight you're going to have fun with your grandparents. I bet they'll even take you for doughnuts in the morning."

"Not exactly a healthy way to start the day," Janis mumbled from where she stood behind Jake.

Jake watched Millie's brow rise and her lips purse.

"We can definitely have doughnuts for breakfast," Janis amended quickly, "if that's what you want, Brooke."

Tipping back her head to kiss Millie's chin, Brooke wrapped her arms awkwardly around her shoulders. "I love you, Fairy Poppins."

"I love you, too, Brookie-Cookie." Millie helped the girl to stand. "Have lots of fun with Nana and Papa so you can tell me all about it when I get back."

Brooke nodded and gave Olivia, then Jake, a hug.

"I'll bring you a doughnut, Daddy."

As he put his arms around her, the fierce need to never let go engulfed him. He straightened and tapped one finger against her nose. "Can you guess my favorite kind?"

"The ones with chocolate icing," Brooke said without hesitation.

"How did you know?" He glanced at Millie, who shook her head.

"Silly, Daddy. Those are my favorites, too."

With that sugary lance to his heart, she took her grandma's hand and skipped out the front door.

* * *

Millie dug her fingernails into the couch cushions to stop herself from bolting into Jake's arms. He looked so stunned and alone as Brooke walked away.

Stop her! Millie wanted to shout. *Don't let her go.*

It was for one night. Millie knew she was overreacting but couldn't help but think there was more to it than that.

Jake turned, his gaze shuttered. "I'm going to get a flashlight and the first-aid kit and have another look at your head."

"I'm fine, Jake." She met her sister's sympathetic gaze and was comforted when Olivia nodded in agreement. "The EMTs said I was fine."

"They said possible concussion."

"You know that's not true."

Finally his eyes met hers. "Humor me on this, Millie." The tenderness in his tone undid her.

She gave a tiny nod. When he'd disappeared down the hall, Millie looked to Olivia. "I'm in trouble here, sis."

"You love him," Olivia supplied.

Millie choked back a sob. "How can I be so stupid? I'm just like my mother, falling for the guy who's my boss. The one I can't have."

"Why can't you have him?"

"Come on, Olivia. This is me. I've told you I don't stick in one place, I don't form long-lasting attachments. I will never have a man dictate my life. Not like she did."

"Jake isn't the type of guy who would want to run your life. The way it looks to me, you do that for him."

"He's also not the type of guy who settles down. And even if he did, it would be for Brooke. They need time. I don't want to get in the way."

"You don't get in the way, Millie. You help bridge the distance between them."

"I can't take the chance if…" She stopped as Jake came back into the room.

"I should go." Olivia stretched her arm around Millie's shoulder and squeezed. "I'm glad you're okay and I'm glad you called me."

"Can I stay with you tonight?" Millie asked as Olivia stood.

She saw Jake stiffen but kept her eyes on Olivia. "Of course," her sister answered slowly. "It probably makes sense since I'll be taking you to Denver for your flight tomorrow morning. I'm just going to step out onto the porch and call Logan. Come on out when you're ready."

When she was alone with Jake, Millie blurted, "I'm sorry. I know I've ruined everything."

"What the hell are you talking about?"

She started to stand but he blocked her, lowering himself to sit behind her. "I want to look at your head."

"It's nothing. I just… The blood… I feel awful that Brooke was scared." She put her fingers to her mouth, emotion welling. "She thought I was dead."

"It was an accident."

"That I should have prevented. I've always had that reaction to blood. If I'd told you and Brooke, she would have known not to be afraid."

"How did she cut her chin?"

His fingers massaged her skin, making some of the tension in her body fade. "She fell off her scooter out front. She was upset that you were late and…"

"Are you saying it was my fault?"

"I didn't mean it that way. I'd set up an obstacle course in the driveway. It's one of the things she loves playing at the preschool. She hit a patch of gravel and fell. I was fine at first, but you know how much blood there can be from even a little cut on the face. I brought her into the house to clean it up and just lost it. It was my fault, Jake. No one else's."

"Sometimes things happen for a reason."

She gave a harsh laugh. "You don't believe that." She turned to him, his hands falling from her head. "I heard you and Janis talking."

"She wants what's best with Brooke."

"So do you."

"That's the point. I'm not best for Brooke. I'm too into my work. Today was a perfect example. I love what I do. I worked my whole life for this career, and I thought I'd lost it. Now I have another chance."

"Does that mean you're going back to work for Miles of Medicine?"

His face went hard. "I told you I would try to be a father. Look at what came of my attempt."

"Because of me," she said on a half sob. "You promised me—"

"I never promised you anything more, Millie."

That stilled her, even as the pain in her heart swelled so savagely she feared it might drag her under. "That's true." *Men don't make promises to people like us, hon.* Her mother's words echoed in her head. *You need to learn to take what you can get and be happy for it.*

She stood, shrugging out of Jake's grasp. "I'm going to my sister's house."

"You don't have to go. You're safe with me. I won't touch you if you don't want me to."

Wasn't that just the problem? She wanted him to touch her almost as much as she wanted to breathe. She could easily push aside her dreams, bury anything she might need in life like her mother had done, just to stay with him.

"I'm leaving, Jake. I'll be in California tomorrow.

When I get back, I'll continue to nanny for you through the end of the month. But I'm staying with Olivia."

"No. Brooke needs you here."

"She needs you here more. Janis was right. You and I are just complicating the situation when we know this isn't going to last."

"How do you know we won't last?"

"Are you staying in Crimson?"

He looked away from her. "I got a job offer from the hospital."

Hope, damned hope, sprang forward in her heart. "Do you plan to accept it?"

He ran his finger through her hair, the unconscious gesture now so familiar and dear to her. "The agency sent a new contract. They want me to go to Africa. There's a huge need because of the drought plaguing the region near Nairobi. I'm good at that kind of medicine. I know I can make a difference there."

I need you to make a difference here. "What are you going to do, Jake?"

"I'm not like your father, Millie. Even if Brooke lives with her grandparents, I won't desert her or put her aside. I'll be a part of her life."

But not mine.

"Do what you think is best, Jake. It's your decision." She made her voice even, belying the emotions that tumbled through her. "This is mine."

Then she stood and walked away.

Chapter Fifteen

"She's not coming back."

"Sure she will, bro. Have a little faith."

Jake glanced at his brother Logan, sitting on the park bench next to him. Brooke called his name and Jake waved to her. She was on the far side of the playground, taking turns on the slide with one of her preschool friends who was also at the park today. Jake caught the eye of the other girl's mother. She waved and went back to texting on her phone.

"Are you afraid that the single-mom vultures will swoop with Millie not around to protect you?"

"I'm afraid of a lot of things." Jake tried to make the words sound like a joke but they held the ominous ring of truth.

"Aren't we all?"

Jake was surprised when his brother didn't try to lighten the conversation. "Olivia's pregnant."

That news broke Jake out of his sour mood. "I'm so

happy for you, Logan." He slapped his brother on the back. "You two will make wonderful parents."

"If it's a girl we're going to name her Elizabeth. We'll call her Liz but I wanted to see what you thought of that?"

"I think Beth would have loved it."

Logan nodded. "I ran into someone I know at the hospital, heard they want you to work for them full-time. We'd love for you to stay in Crimson. Josh, too. Dad has ruled our lives from the great beyond for too long."

Jake didn't like to think of his father involved in any part of his life. "Janis and John are talking about leaving for Atlanta the first part of November. They want to take Brooke with them. The agency needs me in Africa."

"So that's it. You're leaving?"

Jake heard the disappointment in his brother's voice.

"I want to do what's best for Brooke." He dropped his head back, watching the clouds roll by in the bright blue Colorado sky. "I don't believe I'm it, Logan. I'm not cut out to raise a kid on my own."

"If you stay here, you won't be on your own."

"You know what a lot of people in Crimson see when they look at me? Dad."

"That's what you see, not the town."

"I don't want to, but I'm scared as hell that the parts of me that are like him are going to come out and Brooke's going to pay the price."

Logan shook his head. "I wish it wasn't like that for you. You took the brunt of his anger."

"Leaving you, Beth and Josh behind to deal with it when I was gone. I should have done more to make your life a good one. I can do that for my daughter."

"So Brooke and Millie are tossed aside while you move on with your life?" Now Logan sounded angry and Jake felt a matching temper flare to life in himself.

"I didn't create this situation. I'm just trying to deal with it."

"You're not dealing with it." Logan pressed on. "You're running away." He paused then added, "Like you did when you left Crimson the first time." He held up a hand before Jake could argue. "I'm not saying I blame you for going to college, for taking your chance. But you never returned, never tried to stay in contact. You can't forge decent relationships by popping in and out of people's lives, Jake. It didn't work with us and it won't work with your daughter. She needs more."

Brooke waved him over and Jake stood, unable to deal with this conversation any longer. "It's all I have to give, Logan."

By the time he had Brooke settled on the swing, his brother was gone.

Millie did return, true to her word, which should have meant something to him. But it wasn't the same. She barely made eye contact with him each morning as she arrived at the house. She made breakfast, prepped dinner and took care of Brooke's needs. She busied herself in the afternoons when Jake was available with preparations for the fall musical or her plans to return to California. Janis and John stepped in to help as he needed it, and he agreed Brooke would return to Atlanta with them.

A deep ache settled in his chest every time he thought of being separated from Brooke, but Janis tried to convince him that between Skype and phone calls, she and John would make sure he never lost touch with his daughter when he traveled. He'd turned down the job in Crimson and accepted the contract with the agency, wanting to believe he was doing what was best for Brooke.

He hadn't mentioned the plans to her yet. Brooke didn't like Millie staying with Olivia any more than Jake did and had become as clingy and emotional as when he'd first come into her life. He hoped this was just her way of adjusting and scaled back on his shifts at the hospital to spend more time with her.

Each time he did, his heart broke a little. He loved Brooke, but he wanted to do the right thing. No matter what Millie said, being with Jake wasn't it. If it was, why was Millie leaving after the musical?

He'd told her he wanted her to stay with him, that he wouldn't push her for anything she wasn't willing to give. But it hadn't been enough.

It killed him to be near her when all he wanted was to drag her into his arms. He imagined leaving with her and Brooke, venturing deep into the mountains, far away from family and reality. They could be together without the outside world crashing in making demands. Jake had never dealt well with the outside world—that was why he'd always kept to himself and continued his nomadic medical practice.

Was he running the way Logan had suggested? He preferred to think of it as keeping himself sane.

There was certainly no time to reason it all out in Crimson. His brothers and their wives had circled his household like a wagon train. He wasn't sure what Millie had shared with Olivia, but someone was always stopping by or insisting that Jake and Brooke come for dinner.

He was happy that his family had clearly made Millie one of their own, which also meant he had more time with her. Even if he had to watch her across a room or laughing from the other end of the table, he still felt her light travel through him. Sometimes he'd catch her watching him and swore her eyes held the same longing he felt. Then it would be gone and she'd look away.

He didn't blame her. He was making a mess of everything but couldn't see how to stop it.

Two days before the preschool musical, Josh and Logan insisted on a guys' night out. Since both of them were happily married, Jake didn't worry that the evening would turn into a late-night drunkfest, but he still arranged for Brooke to spend the night with Janis and John.

He planned to tell her about his job and the new living arrangements the next morning. He'd put it off as long as he could. He'd come up with all the reasons that this was for the best and how he'd still be a part of her life. Janis and John had agreed to a custody arrangement that would allow Brooke to spend at least a month in the summer and most school holidays with him. He'd explained his new schedule to his boss at the agency. She'd reluctantly agreed, although she was sorry to lose a doctor who'd been willing to travel anywhere in the world with no notice. That wasn't his life anymore. He was doing his best to make things work for everyone involved.

He only wished he knew how to keep Millie involved. He hadn't had a moment alone with her since she'd returned from California. Her sister and friends had seen to that. Jake got the distinct impression that they were protecting her from him but couldn't understand why.

After all, Millie had walked away from *him*.

Thankfully, neither of his brothers brought it up over their dinner at a local hamburger joint. But when they moved on to beers at the Two Moon Saloon, both Josh and Logan were more than willing to tell him how badly he'd mucked up his life—as if he didn't already know.

"I told Sara book smarts don't translate to real life." Josh studied Jake over the rim of his beer bottle. "You never did have a lick of common sense."

"Shut it," Jake growled.

"Olivia's so mad she could spit," Logan added. He punched Jake harder than necessary on the shoulder. "I don't like it when my wife's upset. You know what I mean?"

"I know you both need to let it go." He took a long pull on his beer. "I didn't come back to Crimson to have you two harping at me."

Logan shrugged. "Remind us again—why did you come back? Especially since you're pulling out so soon."

The question threw him. After a few moments he answered, "Because I was scared and overwhelmed. I didn't know how the hell to be a father, what that meant. My only role model had been Dad. You know how that went."

"Bad and worse," Josh answered.

"The past can teach you something about what not to do," Logan agreed.

"We might not have been close, but you two are the only family I have. It made sense to bring Brooke here. Somehow I knew if I needed help, you'd be there for me." He saluted the two of them with his beer bottle. "And you have been."

"So why are you leaving?"

"It's complicated."

"Lame," Logan mumbled.

Jake wanted to lay his fist into his baby brother's face. Before he could argue, his cell phone rang. The display showed John's number. He imagined Brooke wanted to talk to him before she went to bed. He answered and his heart hit the floor as John spoke.

"Call the police," he said, already out of his chair. "I'm on my way."

Josh grabbed at his arm. "What's going on?"

"I need your help. Both of you."

Without hesitation his two brothers stood. Jake would

have been touched except for the ball of fear curling in his gut. "It's Brooke," he said, his voice shaking. "She's gone missing."

Millie stopped at every storefront on the east side of Main Street while Olivia canvassed the other half of the street. Logan had called both Olivia and Millie as he left the bar. Millie hadn't spoken to Jake but knew he must be terrified.

Her stomach had been rolling for the past hour. She and Olivia had raced to Janis and John's rented condo when they found out Brooke had disappeared.

Janis, in between sobs, had told them that they'd tucked Brooke in for bed, but when John had gone to check on her thirty minutes later, she'd been gone.

They turned the house upside down then knocked on each door within a ten-block radius of the house. The police had arrived and started their own search. Neighbors joined in and pretty soon it seemed as if the whole town of Crimson was looking for little Brooke.

Jake had held himself together as he answered questions about his daughter. Millie had wanted to run to him, to apologize for walking out and offer him whatever comfort she could give. But the one time his eyes met hers, he'd looked right through her as if she was no longer alive to him. She'd forced away her own pain, concentrating all her energy on helping find Brooke.

Once Millie and Olivia finished talking to business owners and people on the street, they returned to Jake's house. The makeshift headquarters for the search had been moved there since Janis and John's place didn't have much extra room.

Jake was on his phone when they came into the kitchen. The police had asked him to stay at the house. In case any information came in on the girl, they wanted him to be available.

"No luck?" Katie Garrity asked. She'd closed down the bakery and brought snacks and coffee to the house to keep people going.

Millie shook her head and saw Jake glance her way. She took a step toward him then stopped as his phone clattered to the floor. He moved toward her then past her in a whirlwind.

She turned and saw an older man standing in the doorway to the family room, Brooke sleeping in his arms.

"I think this belongs to you," he said to Jake.

"Brooke." Millie watched as Jake reached forward to take his daughter from the man. He held her close, his shoulders shaking as tears streaked his cheeks.

Brooke snuggled sleepily into her father's chest.

"Silas Benton," Olivia said, walking forward. "How did you end up with this child? You didn't even answer your door when we came by your house."

Silas shrugged. "Found her curled up in a chair on my patio a few minutes ago when I took the dog for his evening walk." He looked at Jake. "I didn't know there was such a big hullabaloo, but I knew right off she was your kid. She's got your eyes, same as your daddy's." He rubbed a hand over his scratchy chin. "Of course, your dad's weren't near so sweet. Always red-rimmed with drink and sharp with temper." He put a hand on Jake's arm. "She looks like you, son."

"Thank you," Jake said, his voice hoarse. Millie saw him wipe at his eyes with the back of his hand before Olivia gave him a tissue.

Again, Millie wanted to go to him but stayed rooted in her place.

Brooke's head lifted. "Daddy, you said you wouldn't leave me."

He kissed the tip of her nose. "You're the one who left, Cookie." He made a broad sweeping motion with his hand. "Half the town was out looking for you tonight."

She glanced over his shoulder to where Janis was seated at the table, silently sobbing. "I heard Nana talking to Papa. They said I was going to live with them. They were making plans for me in Hat-lanta. I don't want to go, Daddy." Her voice rose as she clearly became agitated. "I want to stay with you. I want you to stay with me."

He gave her a tight hug. "I'm not going anywhere and neither are you. We're staying in Crimson, Brooke. You're going to be my girl forever. For as long as you'll have me. There is nothing more important to me than you. I'm sorry it's taken me so long to realize it." He turned to Janis and John. "I know you loved your daughter, and I love mine. Stacy asked me to take care of Brooke for a reason. I'm her father, and it's about time I start acting like it. You're a part of Brooke's life and you always will be. But she belongs with me."

Janis cried harder but nodded. John gave Jake a thumbs-up and came forward to hug his granddaughter.

A round of cheers went up, the loudest from Josh and Logan, who had walked in behind Jake. Millie felt tears spill down her cheeks. This was what she'd wanted from the start. This was the man she knew Jake could be, and it broke her heart even more not to be a part of his world.

Suddenly, the thought of how alone she was settled on her like a heavy burden. As family and friends surrounded Jake, Millie slipped out the back door and walked by herself to Olivia's house.

* * *

They say the show must go on, and the preschool musical was no exception. Millie stood behind the curtain the following night, putting all of the children in their places on the makeshift stage. She gave Brooke an extra hug as she adjusted one of her fox ears.

"I'm so happy you're here, Brookie-Cookie."

Brooke grinned up at her. "Daddy is, too. We're going to live in Crimson. Together. Forever. All of—" The girl broke off and clapped her hand over her mouth.

Millie figured she was worried about breaking Ms. Laura's request for silence before the show started. "It's okay, sweetie. I know just how you feel."

Brooke gave her a curious look but said nothing more. They listened as Ms. Laura thanked the parent volunteers and introduced the program. She made special mention that they were thrilled to have one lost little critter back and Brooke stifled a giggle.

Millie moved offstage as the curtain opened. The parents and family members in the audience watched with smiles and small chortles of laughter as the preschoolers sang and danced their way through the four seasons.

Laura crouched in front of the stage, mouthing words and encouraging the kids. Millie remained out of sight, lining up children for their entrances and giving quick hugs when they exited the stage. Only once did she have to step out when the beaver's costume came down over his eyes and the poor boy underneath started to wander the stage, hands out, as if he were playing a game of Marco Polo.

Brooke sang with gusto through the entire performance, occasionally waving to her family in the front row. Jake sat with his brothers and their wives plus Janis and John. She knew from Olivia that Brooke's grandparents were sorely disappointed the girl wasn't going to live with them, but they seemed to finally understand her devotion to Jake.

Millie took small comfort that she'd known Jake would make a wonderful father. She'd been secretly relieved to hear that Lana Mayfield had taken Jake's open position with Miles of Medicine and had already left Crimson. But someday he'd find a woman to marry, make a proper family and move forward. Likely he'd forget all about her, but she'd always carry with her the knowledge that she'd helped make him and Brooke a family. She may not have had a choice as to her own upbringing, but she was happy to have helped another little girl avoid her same fate.

The audience applauded as the last verse of the song ended. She whispered directions to the children about lining up, then stepped back behind the curtain again.

Laura Wilkes straightened and turned to the audience. She congratulated the children, which led to additional clapping and cheering from the parents.

"I also want to recognize our teaching assistant, Millie Spencer, for all the time and energy she's put into making our musical a success."

Another round of applause sounded as Laura turned and motioned Millie to join her at the front. Millie shook her head, but the clapping grew louder. Then Brooke walked over and took her hand, leading her out from behind the curtain.

Millie wasn't used to being the center of attention this way. Her knees trembled as she smiled and nodded at the parents in the audience. After being run out on the rails from her last teaching position, the change here was overwhelming to her senses.

As the audience quieted, Laura gave her a small hug. "You've been such a blessing to this preschool," she said, her voice gentle. "I wish there was something we could do to convince you to stay on in Crimson."

One of the boys from the class stepped forward and handed Millie a stack of letters, tied with a ribbon.

"Thank-you notes from the class," Laura explained.

"Read mine now," Brooke said, bouncing on her toes next to Millie. "I made it special today." She handed Millie a folded piece of paper.

Millie could feel color rise to her cheeks. "This is so nice," she said to Laura. "All of it. You didn't have to—"

"Read my letter." Brooke snatched the paper from her hand, opened it and held it up in front of Millie. The crowd fell silent. In bold, childish scrawl were the words *Merry Us*.

A sigh went up in the crowd, but Millie stood in confusion for a few seconds as Brooke stared at her expectantly.

"It should be an *A*," a voice from the audience said. As she turned, Jake walked up the few steps to stand in front of her. His smile was hesitant, unsure and so very sweet to her.

"So will you with an *A*?" Brooke asked.

"Will I—"

"Marry us?" Jake supplied. "Or more specifically, marry me?"

"Daddy, do it right." Brooke poked at her father's leg. "You have to do it right so she'll say yes."

He took a breath, as if to calm his nerves, and dropped to one knee. He slid his fingers into hers, and despite all of the people watching, Millie couldn't look away from his gaze.

"I love you, Millie," he said softly.

"Speak up," someone from the audience yelled. Millie

was pretty sure the voice belonged to Josh. "They can't hear you in the back."

"I love you," Jake said more clearly, not taking his eyes from hers. "I think I loved you from the first moment you came shimmering into my life. You changed things. You brought back laughter and light and you helped me become the man I didn't know I could be."

"You were always that man," she whispered.

He shook his head. "It's because of you. It's for you. You deserve so much more than I can ever give you, Millie. But please let me try. I want you to be my wife."

"And my stepmom," Brooke added.

Jake drew his daughter to his side. "We're a package deal, Brooke and me. But we won't be whole without you in our lives. Please marry us."

Stunned, Millie looked out to the audience then to the preschoolers watching from the stage. She'd come to think of this place as home but never imagined she could feel as happy and complete as she did at this moment.

"You gonna say yes or no?" one of the boys asked. "'Cause if you don't want him, I'll marry you."

Millie let out a laugh. "Yes," she said, as Jake stood, picked up Brooke and wrapped them both in a tight hug. "I love you. I love you both. Of course I'll marry you, Jake. You're my heart and my life."

The crowd cheered again. Millie buried her face in Jake's shoulder, afraid that her emotions would get the best of her.

Laura Wilkes spoke again. "Let's celebrate our preschoolers and this new engagement with cake and punch out on the back lawn."

This time the cheer went up from the children. Brooke wiggled out of Jake's grasp and led the charge out the door.

Jake wrapped both his arms around Millie and pulled her to the back of the stage behind the curtain.

"You're sure?" he asked, tipping up her chin. "You'll have me even though I'm the biggest idiot on the planet?"

She smiled and touched her hand to his cheek. "You're mine and you're not an idiot," she whispered and reached onto her tiptoes to kiss him. "We're going to figure this out together, Jake. I love you and there's no place in the world I'd rather be than at your side."

He deepened the kiss and her senses spun. She reveled in the heat of him around her and the love she'd always dreamed of having.

"Forever, Millie. You are mine. Forever."

Just then the curtain pulled back. Brooke stood there, a fork in her hand, icing smeared across her cheek. "Come on, you guys." She shook the fork at them. "Uncle Josh and Uncle Logan are going to eat all the cake if you don't hurry."

"Then let's go," Jake said, ruffling his daughter's hair, and the three of them walked into the future together.

Epilogue

One Month Later

"Are you sure you're okay to leave Bunny behind?" Millie bent forward to readjust one of the flowers that adorned Brooke's hair.

The little girl nodded. "He doesn't like weddings and ate too much pumpkin pie yesterday. I'll put him down for a nap and then we can get married." She giggled at the words she'd just said. "I mean you can get married. To Daddy."

As Brooke went to adjust her stuffed animal on the bed, Millie turned to Olivia, who smiled at the two of them from where she stood near the door, holding a bouquet of pale lilies. "Thank you for arranging all of this so quickly."

"It was my pleasure. I'm happy for you, Millie."

"But with your condition…"

"I feel great, hardly any morning sickness." Olivia

patted her stomach, which was just beginning to round. "Besides, Sara and Natalie helped. Katie took care of all the food. It was a community effort." Her smile widened. "It helped that you and Jake wanted a small wedding. You're absolutely radiant."

Millie looked at herself in the mirror above the dresser. She was getting married today. Her heart pounded as she tried to absorb the significance of that.

Josh and Sara had insisted they have the ceremony at Crimson Ranch, so she was in one of the guest bedrooms at the main house. It was Thanksgiving Day. They'd decided to hold the wedding on the holiday that was traditionally filled with family and food, keeping things easy and casual for everyone involved. Millie had been staying with Olivia and Logan since Jake had asked her to marry him because they didn't want to confuse Brooke with the change in Millie's status from nanny to future stepmother.

Like Brooke, her hair was adorned with tiny flowers, and the simple white dress with a lace overlay made her feel like a true bride. The engagement ring Jake had given her sparkled on her finger. The stone was a beautiful yellow diamond surrounded by a cluster of smaller clear diamonds. He'd told her he always wanted her to remember that she'd brought color and sunshine into his life. Every time she looked at the ring and what it represented, her heart sang.

"It's happiness," Millie whispered. "I look happy."

"You do, indeed. Even your mom noticed."

"I can't believe she came. I didn't think she'd make the trip."

"She loves you," Olivia told her. "She might not have been the greatest mom growing up, but she does love you."

Millie turned and walked toward her sister, reaching forward to give Olivia a swift hug. "I know your mom loves you, as well, even though the thought of me gives her hives." She squeezed her sister's shoulders. "I think Dad loved all of us in his own convoluted way."

"I'm glad you're staying in Crimson, Millie. You belong here. I always wanted a big family—"

"Me, too."

"Now we both have one." Olivia wiped at her eyes.

"Don't make me cry," Millie said with a laugh. "My makeup will run."

A soft tap sounded on the door and Sara poked her head in. "The guys are ready." Her gazed landed on Millie and she waved her hand in front of her face. "You look so perfect it's going to make me cry."

"No happy tears until the wedding," Olivia whispered.

"Right," Sara agreed. "I'll tell them you're ready to start?"

Millie took a deep breath and nodded. "It's time."

Sara closed the door again as Brooke came up to take Millie's hand. "Let's go get married so you can come home."

Millie couldn't agree more and followed the girl she loved like a true daughter into the hall.

Jake watched Brooke walk down the makeshift aisle in the big Crimson Ranch family room. Furniture had been moved so that chairs could be set in front of the picture window overlooking the valley. A dusting of early snow covered the highest peaks, a sure sign the seasons were changing in Crimson. Jake stood before the window, flanked by Logan, who was serving as his best man, and Josh, who'd agreed to officiate the service. They'd been looking for an officiate when someone in town had mentioned the little-known Colorado law that allowed Jake and Millie to perform the marriage ceremony themselves or have someone in the wedding party do it. Josh had offered, which seemed like a perfect fit for the intimate gathering they wanted.

It was only family and close friends in the room, but his daughter dropped her rose petals with the pomp and circumstance fit for a royal wedding.

He couldn't imagine that a few short months ago he hadn't even known she existed. She'd turned his tired world upside down and made him want to overcome his fears to be the father she deserved. He would always be grateful to Stacy for allowing him the opportunity to be a part of his daughter's life and wouldn't forget what she'd sacrificed in the process.

Olivia came into view next. He heard Logan draw in a breath and glanced over to see his youngest brother break into an ear-to-ear grin at the sight of his pregnant wife. Jake was happy Logan had come through his grief over their sister's death and knew Olivia was to thank for it.

Then Millie appeared in the doorway and every thought other than her vanished. She gave him a shy smile as she walked toward him. The combination of her delicate wedding gown, the flowers woven into her hair and the way her skin shimmered in the light made her truly look like a fairy come to life. But Millie was a real woman and Jake could barely believe that she was about to become his forever.

"She's wearing the lotion I like." Brooke tugged on his hand. "She's glittery, Daddy. Like when we first met her."

He lifted his daughter into his arms and gave her a hug. "She is beautiful inside and out. Just like you, Cookie."

"You got the ring, right?"

"It's right here," Logan said from Jake's side. He reached out for Brooke. "Come here, sweetie. You can help me keep it safe."

Brooke allowed herself to be transferred to Logan's arms. Jake concentrated on Millie walking down the aisle. When she got close enough he stepped forward and took her hands in his. "I love you," he whispered. "Now and forever, Millie."

"Forever," she repeated.

Josh cleared his throat from behind Logan. "You two are stealing my thunder. This may be the first and last wedding I officiate. Let me have a little fun here."

Millie laughed as she and Jake turned to his brother.

The ceremony was very personal for the two of them. Sara and Natalie each read a poem. Then Jake recited the vows he'd written for Millie.

He felt his palms grow damp as he looked into her eyes. Jake wasn't the kind of guy who talked about his feelings, but he wanted Millie and everyone in the room to understand exactly how he felt about her. "From the moment I met you, my life changed for the better. You are so much more than I ever expected. More intelligent, more caring, more beautiful. I want to spend the rest of my life building a life with you. I can't promise there won't be difficult times, but I will promise to stay by your side through every moment. Now and forever."

Millie's eyes shone with tears by the time he finished. "You may not say much, Dr. Travers, but you sure know how to make the words count when you do."

He took the ring Brooke handed him and slipped the thin wedding band onto her finger. "I don't ever want you to doubt my love, Millie."

She shook her head. "I wouldn't. I love you, Jake. All my life I've been looking for a home, for a place I could truly belong. I've found that with you. At your side, I'm so much better than on my own. I want you as my partner, my friend and my one true love. No matter what the future brings, we'll face it together. Now and forever."

Josh pronounced them husband and wife and Jake took her in his arms. This was where the two of them belonged, together with their family and friends, building the life they both wanted.

Now and forever.

* * * * *

0615/23